PINK NEON

MEGAN STOCKTON

Bad Luck Cat Publishing

Printed in the United States of America

First Printing, 2025

Any references to historical events, real people, or real places are used fictitiously.

Editing by Dagan Boyd

Cover artwork by Dagan Boyd

Printed and produced using KDP, an Amazon Platform.

Bad Luck Cat Publishing

Grimsley, TN

https://www.meganstocktonbooks.com

"You're killing people."

"No, I'm killing boys."

- Jennifer's Body (2009)

One

"Come on, baby doll," Tansi whispered, voice sounding wet and gravelly in her throat as she struggled to drag the other woman up the stairs. "Come on."

The woman's head lolled, rolling around on her shoulders as her tailbone struck every stair on the way up with a soft thunk. Tansi wished there was a better way, she knew that this would be painful for Alice later, but right now, she could see no other way. There was only one more small flight of stairs to ascend before they reached the floor of her apartment. On the landing, Alice vomited, gurgling like a clogged drain, before a stream of sour liquid erupted from around her flaccid lips. Tansi paused long enough to quickly roll her onto her side, patting her back as she tried to make sure she didn't inhale too much of the vomit.

She took a deep breath, holding the back of her wrist to her mouth and nose as she tried to avoid the smell. It smelled like gastric juice more than anything else, but also the smell of something savory and rich. The only thing her mind could think of was the brown gravy served with Thanksgiving dinner. She couldn't remember the last time she'd enjoyed a Thanksgiving dinner, and now she wasn't sure she could ever stomach turkey gravy again.

She picked Alice up under the arms, forced to drag her through the pile of wet vomit, leaving a streak of filth across the floor and residue on every stair. She was covered in it, her shirt soaked through. The thin yellow fabric clung to her navel and breasts, making them visible in the damp.

Thank God Alice's apartment wasn't far down the hall from the top of the stairs. Tansi fumbled through the woman's pockets to find her key, jamming it into the lock and jiggling the knob as she pushed and twisted at the same time. The damn thing was always so fucking sticky. It was easy enough to open from the inside, but God forbid you ever need to get inside in a hurry from the hallway.

It finally gave way, dragging against the tight carpet on the interior. It was slightly frizzy and fluffy from the continuous contact of the door's base, making a little snagging noise like a corroded zipper as it allowed her to drag Alice the rest of the way inside.

The interior of the studio apartment was stained pink from the neon signs on the streets outside: fuschia and black battling for purchase in every unlit corner.

She dragged the unconscious woman into the dingy yellow bathroom. The overhead light was the same hue as pale butter, accentuating the off-color walls. The tile floor had once been white, but now it was dusty grey with plentiful lint sticking to the grout and mold speckling the union of floor and wall.

Hoisting them both into the shower, she cranked on the cold water, holding Alice's body against her own as she let the water pour over them. Her skin was still hot to the touch, like the recently used surface of a stove.

"You're gonna cook," Tansi whispered, shivering as the water drenched her hair. Swirls of the black and purple strands stuck to her face like cryptic tattoos as she clutched Alice tightly, pressing her fingertips against her chest to try and feel her pounding heart: a confirmation of life.

Her hands grazed a crucifix on a dainty chain that Alice kept tucked deep into her bra, making tiny indentations on the inside of each breast where the metal rested between her cleavage and gently bit in.

"God, if you're here now..." Tansi paused, voice a hushed whisper. "If you're here, please don't look."

Two

Tansi didn't sleep much, just dozing off and on as she sat in the bed beside Alice's sleeping form. Her skin had cooled down and she had finally stopped throwing up, but the mattress was still damp with sweat. It was late in the morning, approaching afternoon, but Tansi didn't dare leave her for more than just a few seconds at a time.

Alice was her lifeline. When Tansi found herself out here with no money to her name, chasing the dream of being an escort to rich men in fancy hotels, bathing in champagne and wiping her ass with hundred dollar bills... God, she'd been so naive and hopeful. Part of her wanted to blame Alice for introducing her to the underbelly of the shining dragon she had pursued so willingly. Without Alice taking her in, letting her live rent free with her in her apartment, and showing her the ropes and how to handle tricks, she could've wound up dead somewhere.

The front door to the apartment pushed open, dragging across the carpet with a snag, and a young girl appeared: once purple hair now faded to a lilac-blue, dark circles nearly the same color under her eyes. She had two grocery bags in her hands, which she promptly set on the countertop when she entered.

"Hey, Luce," Tansi whispered, raising a hand in greeting.

Lucy kicked off her white sneakers by the door, walking slowly over the carpet in her dingy socks. It was something she always did when she came into the apartment: shoes immediately off and placed by the door. When they say "old habits die hard," no one ever thinks about the little mannerisms ingrained from childhood..

"What's up?" she asked, sitting carefully on the edge of the mattress.

"I don't know, she took something last night. She could barely walk, but she seemed fine, you know? By the time we got down the street, I was dragging her. Literally dragging her. She was so hot that I could barely touch her. Like a stove eye, I swear to God! Kept throwing up. I put her in a cold shower and then when she was cooled off, I put her in the bed. I've watched her all night, though – kept her turned on her side."

Lucy reached out to grab Tansi's hands, squeezing them with a smile. "She'll be alright. You did all the right things. Molly'll do that to you."

Alice stirred and then sat up with a groan. Her face was speckled pink behind her freckles, a tinge of blue still rimming her pale lips. She sniffled, although her nose sounded dry, and turned to look at Tansi.

"Grab me a shirt, if you can."

Alice had one of those silky, sultry voices that people loved. She sounded like she was whispering even when she was speaking with volume; every word had a sort of wispy quality that made it hard to discern whether it was an accented twang or a speech impediment.

Tansi grabbed an oversized t-shirt from the top drawer without even checking to see who it belonged to and tossed it to Alice, along with a pair of comfortable underwear. She settled back down on the bed beside her as she slipped both articles on.

"How you feeling, hon'?" Lucy asked with a soft smile.

Alice put two manicured fingers to her forehead and returned the smile. "Alright, just partied a little too hard, I guess. I don't even remember how I got here. My back is killing me."

"I had to drag your ass up here," Tansi reminded her. "The guys dropped us off on the corner and you never opened your eyes. They set you up against the Flamingo and took off."

"Those assholes."

Lucy wandered over to the sink and turned on the faucet. The water gurgled and spurted a rust-stained stream before it purified in clarity. She retrieved a glass from the cabinet and filled it halfway with the tap water before she brought it over to Alice and put it into her hands carefully. Tansi watched her drink the sulfury, iron-rich water like it was a shot of alcohol: throwing it back and wincing as it descended to her gut.

"What time is it?" Alice cleared her throat.

"It's probably noon, I'd say."

"I've got to meet DJ. I was supposed to be there an hour ago; he's going to be fucking pissed."

As Alice got to her feet, finding a pair of comfortable yoga pants and pulling them on with little grace to speak of, Tansi followed.

"Do you need me to go with you? You still seem a little unsteady."

Alice didn't respond immediately, rolling the top inch of the waistband down to more securely fit on her hips. Tansi gave her time to consider the offer. She knew the only reason Alice would go see DJ – aside from turning in her dues for the week – would be to get her fix. Everybody had their demons, and Alice's was drugs. She had been adamant about trying to keep Tansi from using, and helping Lucy to get clean, but she never faced her own addiction head on. She leaned into it.

"Yeah, sure. Won't be long," she finally responded.

Tansi matched Alice's vibe with a set of comfortable clothes and followed her out the door. Lucy had helped herself to a tub of vanilla ice cream and stuck the spoon against her tongue before waving at them as they left the apartment.

The apartment building where the girls lived was, ironically, titled "The Palace." Once upon a time, maybe it was some ritzy sort of establishment, but those days were long gone. Every floor had water-damaged ceilings with creeping black mold dotting the corners. The carpet was darkening with debris and use, and the old light fixtures in the hallway were reminiscent of an old mansion, but they didn't work anymore. It was built slightly elevated from street level, on a small rise in the side of a hill.

Rent was cheap, though, and that's what most people who lived on Jessop Terrace needed.

Jessop Terrace, or "The Strip," as many called it, was one of the oldest parts of town. While most of the city was very modern and drew in a lot of successful people and wide-eyed youth with big aspirations, The Strip was where hope and dreams went to die.

When the region had relied on coal mining, this was the part of town where all of the shops and stores had been. It was where people *wanted* to be. The buildings here had very simple addresses: 1 through 12 Jessop Terrace. Instead of alternating even on one side and odd on another, the north side was 1 through 6, and the south side was 7 through 12.

Directly across from The Palace was the life of the party: a gay bar called the Flaming-O and a strip club called Pink Panther. Graffiti above Pink Panther's street number of "2" read TWO IN THE PINK, and above the Flaming-O's "1" read ONE IN THE STINK.

People thought they were hilarious.

"He's at home," Alice mentioned as they started down the street.

DJ frequented the strip club and was in tight with the owner, Donnie. Sometimes DJ supplied girls for more intimate sessions, and while they counted cash together, they'd make jokes about women like they were trading cards and about being pimps like it was a coveted elected office.

"I might wait outside, if that's good with you." Tansi mentioned quietly as they approached the apartment building at the end of the street.

If Tansi could avoid seeing DJ, she did at all costs. Sometimes she would send her dues with Alice; other times DJ was too busy and would send his bottom bitch to get the money for him. If she could meet him at Pink Panther, she did, but she would do anything to keep from stepping foot inside his apartment.

"That's up to you," Alice responded, voice quiet. She was still so pale, and her hands quivered as she reached to press the call button at the apartment door.

DJ's voice came across the speaker: "Yeah?"

"Hey, it's me," Alice responded.

"You're really fucking late."

"I'm sorry, Deej. Something came up."

"Yeah, well sit on whatever came up and fuck off."

Alice leaned towards the speaker desperately. "Please."

There was a long pause. "Alright. Well, it's going to cost you."

Tansi watched Alice's face stiffen, and her stomach sank. DJ was a real asshole. She wasn't sure she could fight him off if he tried to beat on Alice, but she was willing to try. He controlled the girls by feeding their addictions when he could, and when he couldn't, he wasn't afraid to intimidate with physical violence. He called them all family, but it was always about *control*.

The door buzzed and Alice headed inside, and Tansi jumped from her place against the wall to slip in behind her.

"Thought you was going to wait outside?" Alice asked.

"Nah, you aren't leaving me out there by myself – are you crazy? Creeps everywhere, even in the daylight." She offered a supportive smile as they started up the stairs.

DJ was standing at his open door when they mounted the third landing. The whites of his eyes were red, and his pupils were blown out; he had dried blood flecked below his nose. His greasy black hair was pulled back into a matted and frizzy ponytail. They weren't the only ones who'd experienced a rough night, by the looks of it.

Alice had a thin sheen of glittering sweat on her brow, and her pallor had become even more significant. He sidestepped to allow them inside, eyes following them both with the calculating intensity of a predator. Tansi kept her spine straight and her eyes forward, forcing her features into the softness of apathy.

DJ shut the door behind them, latching the door chain and the deadbolt before he pushed past them and opened a box. Alice fidgeted with the hem of her shirt, twisting a string around the first joint of her finger until it turned white. DJ returned with a small plastic baggie between his index and middle finger, offering it to Alice. She reached up to grab it, but he snatched his wrist away from her before leaning in.

"I told you... you have to pay for it."

DJ's eyes wandered to Tansi as he continued a slow tilt to advance his mouth near Alice's ear.

"Suck my dick."

She saw Alice's jaw tense and her throat pulse with a dry swallow before she reached up to pull her hair back. As she started to get onto her knees he looked down at her.

"Not you."

Tansi felt a nervousness creep into her chest, and then down into her gut. It wasn't that she had an issue with giving a guy head. She did that every day. It was the principal. This wasn't a transaction, this was a punishment.

"She doesn't owe you anything." Alice said, voice shaking.

"You're right, but it'll make you think twice about making me wait again won't it? I make sure you get what you need, and all I ask is that you make me some money and you don't waste my time. Not to mention you look like *shit*. You sick or something?"

Alice looked back at Tansi, but the look on her face wasn't what she had expected to see. It was sympathetic: apologetic for what she had to do. What she *wanted* her to do so she could get her fix. Addiction did possess you with all the persuasive power of a demonic entity.

Her expression became desperate and pleading with Tansi's hesitation.

"Okay," she breathed.

DJ reached down to unfasten his belt, popping the button of his blue jeans loose, modest beer gut forcing the zipper down of its own volition. Alice backed away, and Tansi heard her heels strike the kitchen island.

"You stay right there and watch," DJ commanded, flicking the bag of dense powder in her direction.

Tansi got onto her knees as he pulled his dick out of his pants and pressed the sticky tip to her lips so hard that she felt it against her teeth. He slowly wound his hand through her hair, damp and sweaty palm snagging against the strands, fingertips pressing deep against her scalp.

"I'll be quick," he said, and she looked up at him to see him rubbing his fingers along his gums as he ground his gold teeth together.

She put him into her mouth and ran her tongue around the head of his penis, finding a ring of crusted fluid underneath: a rim of salty, bitter crystals that left a grit on her teeth like a disgusting martini glass.

The hand in her hair grabbed tightly at the back of her head and drew her forward with so much force that her neck popped. She slid her tongue along his shaft, her eyes watering as he pressed himself deeper into her throat. She closed her eyes and went somewhere else. Sometimes she spent all of the time cycling through memories like the reel of a viewfinder; other times she went straight to a happy place.

Sometimes it was a mundane place: a rainy day in the back of a cab, chewing a piece of cool peppermint, inhaling the cold winter air through her nostrils and letting it chill her menthol-teased palate. A kind-voiced man in a bowler hat sat behind the wheel, calling her sweetie, listening to George Strait love songs on the radio's lowest possible audible volume.

THREE

WHEN NIGHT FELL, THE Strip twinkled awake with hellish light. It cast an ominous pink hue across the street that somehow made the shadows more pronounced, burning images of cars, shapes of street signs, and silhouettes of faceless men into Tansi's brain like she was looking into the sun.

She stumbled out of a long black car. The sidewalk approached her feet quicker than she anticipated and her ankle turned to jelly atop her high-heeled shoe.

"See you next week, huh?" the man asked from the driver's seat; she responded by slamming the door with her ass. She heard him chuckle, and she readjusted her clutch bag on her shoulder as she strutted down the street with her sore ankle towards Alice and Lucy.

Alice was propped up against a streetlight, smoking a joint as she stared off into space. Her cheeks looked so sunken in the contrast of the shadows that she could've been a corpse.

"How's you guys doing?" Tansi asked, combing her fingers through the sticky ends of her hair before wiping a little bit of rogue cum on the base of her dress.

Lucy leaned towards her, arms crossed over her chest. "I got something to tell you two. What do you say we take the night off early, and I'll make dinner?"

Alice suddenly came alive, looking down at her with furrowed brows. "I got a big quota to meet this week. I can't slip up right now; I'm on thin ice. DJ is going to cut me off if I don't walk the line."

"You ain't left this spot all night, Alice," Lucy said flatly. "Every john that comes by you're pawning off on me or Tansi."

Alice took a long drag from the emaciated joint, more paper than substance, and then flicked it into the storm drain. She blew the smoke straight into the air, her black wig tipping crookedly. She was in no state to be out here right now. She was going to piss someone off.

"Alright," Tansi answered for her. "We can take off early. I did good tonight, had a couple of regulars. It's early in the week anyway. I could go for some food."

Lucy's knees bounced, and she clapped her hands, eyes lighting up as she led them down the street to the apartment. They didn't speak until they were inside, slowly climbing the stairs together.

"You ever looked at those house ads in the paper? You know the one where they show all the fancy places for sale in town?"

"I don't look at what I can't afford," Alice responded, "but, yeah... yeah, I know what you're talking about."

"I saw a real nice place the other day. Had like a little yard and everything. I cut it out and keep it in my purse now."

Tansi smiled a little. "You're so funny, Luce."

"It ain't funny; I am speaking it into existence. You know, *manifesting*."

"I'm gonna manifest a beach house in Cabo, a butler, and my own personal Bradley Cooper. You think they got pics of those in the paper?"

The girls laughed.

"What about you, Tansi?" Lucy asked, voice bubbly.

"I'd just want a small place, away from all the noise. Maybe a little house in Last Bend."

The laughter subsided. It wasn't as funny when you just wanted to live in the place you'd run away from in the first place. She didn't want to go back to her own past, though. Tansi just wanted *home*, but without all the heartache and pain... if there was such a thing.

They left the final set of stairs for their floor, walking down the hall, led by Alice as she fumbled for the key in her purse. A heavy-set man with a mullet and a grease-stained wife beater was standing with his door open. The television blared a sports broadcast behind him.

He smiled at them when they approached, tucking his thumbs into his waistband.

"Ladies! Taking the night off early, huh? I know you gotta be dying for a little action in your downtime. You know, I wouldn't charge you a thing if you wanna come in and hang out."

Lucy stopped in the hall, turning to square up with the man straight on. It wasn't their first encounter with him; he was always a creep. Lucy was the sweetest, bounciest young woman... until she wasn't. She could be absolutely venomous.

She looked him up and down once, tossing her hair out of her face.

"Yeah, like I'm just dying to suck your nasty cock after it's fermented in your shorts with your sweaty ballsack all fucking day. When's the last time you washed your asshole? Because I can tell you from here it ain't recent enough."

"Oh, fuck off, you nasty cunt," he said, face transitioning from red to purple. He spat onto the floor and retreated into his apartment as Lucy pursued, spitting her own wad of saliva onto the 314 on his door.

Tansi followed Alice into the apartment, and Lucy hurried in behind them.

"Just have a seat. I'll take care of everything," Lucy said, pulling off her heels and tossing them to the floor before she went to the sink and washed her hands.

Tansi took more time to remove her own shoes, unzipping her dress and letting it fall into a shimmering ring of fabric on the floor. She put on a pair of panties and a t-shirt, seating herself at the bar. Alice didn't take off anything other than her wig before she sat down, scratching her short-cropped, dark hair underneath.

Lucy was in the freezer, pulling out boxes of frozen Chinese food: Schezwan chicken, fried rice, egg rolls, noodles. She preheated the oven and put a skillet on every stove eye.

Tansi exchanged a confused glance with the exhausted Alice and then cleared her throat. She wasn't sure if she should be amused or concerned about Lucy's excited busyness.

"Hungry, Luce?" Tansi inquired.

She didn't respond immediately, oiling the pans and emptying the contents of each bag into its respective pan. She put the egg rolls into the still-cold oven as she started sauteeing the food on the stove. Tansi was antsy now. Being patient had never been one of her strong suits, and paranoia was one of her vices. She had an intense need to *know* and *understand* everything immediately. It was something that should have driven her to success in college, but instead had her dropping out because she couldn't handle the stress and responsibility.

The apartment filled with the aroma of the food, and Tansi's stomach rolled. She found herself leaning over the island to watch as Lucy put a generous serving of everything except the egg rolls onto the plates and brought it over to them. Alice poked around at her food with a fork, using the tines to pick up a single grain of rice and place it between her teeth. Tansi took forkfuls at a time, savoring every flavor.

"So," Lucy said, "like I said, I got big news. Are you ready?"

"Did you win the lottery?" Alice asked with a smile.

"Sort of," Lucy said, turning sideways and pulling the sides of her flowy top back. "I'm pregnant."

Tansi stopped, a rogue noodle still hanging from her lips. She had to make the decision to snip it off with her teeth and let it fall to the plate, or to slurp it awkwardly down in the silence. She chose the latter, sauce splattering onto her nose as she looked over at Alice.

"Well, that's just—" Alice started. "Whose baby is it?"

Tansi hadn't stopped staring at Lucy's slim form. She didn't *look* pregnant. She was tiny. She couldn't remember the last time she'd seen a pregnant woman. When did they start showing?

"I can't tell you right now, not until I tell him anyway.... You'll just have to trust me, but he's going to take care of us. I know he makes the money, and I know he cares about me and..."

"Lucy..." Alice said, voice soft. It was the "mom" voice. She began slowly rising to her feet, but Lucy held a finger in the air, jabbing it towards Alice in a sharp motion.

In an instant, the young woman's eyes welled with tears.

"Don't," she warned.

Despite the threat, Alice continued, "If this guy is a trick, you know you can't talk to him about being pregnant or you'll get in serious trouble. DJ will flip his shit. It's bad business."

"We just care about you, Luce," Tansi offered gently, reaching across the counter with her palm up. "This is no place for a baby. What are you gonna do? DJ isn't gonna just let you go off and play house."

"I have saved up more money than I ever owed DJ for anything – and more than that! A little bonus for keeping me in work all this time. The guy's not a john, and he's gonna get us out of here after I talk to DJ. I know he will. He told me he loved me, you know. He's different."

Tansi retracted her rejected hand, and for a few minutes, they sat in silence with Lucy, who had taken to spearing chunks of chicken aggressively with a fork. She was holding back tears; Tansi could tell by the way her hands quivered and the way she blinked only when absolutely necessary.

Lucy had been in the life since she was a kid. Her story wasn't that unusual: she had run away from a broken home with an abusive daddy and a deadbeat mama. Got hooked on drugs, specifically heroin, then a knight in shining armor showed up: DJ. He wooed her, became her too-old boyfriend who kept her spoon warm and shared her with his friends for money. It was the easiest way to integrate her into the life. By the time she realized she wasn't special and that she was just another means to gain a few dollars, it probably felt like it was too late.

"You still using?" Tansi asked, trying to keep her tone from sounding accusatory.

"I'm clean. I've been clean. I've been doing really good – I don't even *want* to use no more. I'm going to be a good mom, Tansi."

"You'll be a great mom," Alice confirmed. She made eye contact with Lucy, who grinned back at her. Her entire demeanor changed.

"How far along are you?" Tansi chimed in, trying to fake her own smile.

"I haven't been to the baby doctor yet, but I'd say twenty-something weeks. I kind of waited to tell you guys... just wanted to be sure it was going to last, you know."

"Just be careful, alright?"

Alice added, "Be *smart*."

Lucy ignored them, raising her head to sniff the air. The egg rolls were burning.

Four

Tansi normally avoided the white Honda when it rolled down The Strip, but tonight was different. She crossed her arms over her chest as Alice disappeared into a man's car, and then she watched the Honda roll to a stop, a few other working girls crowding the window. Tansi waited until they left and then started walking down the street with a purpose.

The driver must have seen her coming, because the car remained parked by the curb, burning oil in a cloud of white smoke, stained pink. She approached the window slowly, crouching down to make eye contact with the woman inside.

She was wearing an emerald-green dress suit that was bright against her dark skin. A well-manicured hand with long nails grasped the steering wheel, and the other fumbled for a brown paper bag on the floorboard.

"You finally decide to come talk to me?" the woman asked with a laugh. "Better late than never, sweetheart. Got a bag right here for you. Clean needles, condoms, a candy bar, and a brochure for my outreach program in case you ever wanna—"

"I don't need any of that," Tansi said quickly, cutting her off.

The woman paused, puzzled. She held the little bag in her hand for a moment before setting it down in the seat beside her. She didn't look angry, though; she seemed curious and maybe a little concerned.

"What can we do for you, babydoll?" she asked.

Tansi found herself crossing her arms again, looking both ways down the street to be sure no one witnessed the conversation. Speaking to this lady wasn't like talking to a cop or a social worker, but a lot of the pimps hated how nosy this lady was. There'd been discussion of trying to scare her away – or worse – but no one ever did anything. Rumor was that she had been in the life before, too, and now she advocated for girls like her. Maybe that's why the guys hated her: she represented a threat to the longevity of business.

"I got a friend... she might need some help."

"Your friend got a name?"

Tansi hesitated, and the lady held a finger to her lips. "I would never do anything to jeopardize your girls."

She wanted to tell her that just *being* here was jeopardizing them, and that she should know that. But instead, she went against her instincts.

"Lucy."

"That her real name or her street name?"

"I only know anybody by their street name, and everybody only knows me by mine. That's how things work out here."

"I know how things work out here," she confirmed with an edge to her voice. "What kind of problem is your friend having?"

"She's pregnant."

"We can get her into an abortion clinic," the lady said, retrieving a business card and handing it out the window to Tansi. It read: *Keistyn Ferrarese*, CEO and Founder, fEmpower: Advocacy Program for At-Risk Women and Girls.

"And if she wants, like... prenatal care instead?"

Keistyn looked at Tansi for a long moment and sighed. "Try to get her to reach out to me. Let me help her."

"Can you get her out of here? Like... if she wants out of the life?"

"If she wanted out, she'd be asking me herself, wouldn't she?"

"Not that easy, I don't think."

"Give her the card. I'll do whatever I can. If I can get a girl out, I'll get a girl out. Be safe out there. You sure you don't want a bag?"

Tansi took the bag with great resistance and didn't have time to say thank you before Keistyn took off down the street. She sometimes fooled the girls into wandering over – if they didn't recognize her – the way she cruised with the window cracked, pausing next to each body that stood there.

Almost instantly, another car came up beside her and rolled down the window. There was a man: middle aged, average in every way. He had a pressed shirt and a tan line on his finger that Tansi thought probably suggested he was married. Most of these men were. Two-and-a-half kids, picket fence, golden retriever. Some naive old lady waiting for them at home, thinking they were working late or stuck in traffic. Spending their lunch money on something naughty, like boys buying cigarettes on a playground.

She remembered the first guy she'd turned after Alice dropped her into the middle of this vile world. The man had looked at her, but not like she had ever really been used to being looked at. He looked at her like he wasn't looking at another person. It was like she was something on a shelf that he had the urge to slip into his pocket and steal. It was like she didn't really *have a say*. She wasn't scared at that moment, although maybe she should have been intimidated by his predatory gaze. Instead of feeling powerless, however, she felt *powerful*.

Just like she did now. She was in control and she had something he wanted; she had something he needed. She had something he was paying for.

"Hey, honey," she said with a smile, sauntering over to lean down into the car.

She thought he was going to be easy, the way his eyes instantly fell to her meager cleavage and then rose to her lips. She smiled again.

"You looking for some company?"

He pulled a bill out of his pocket and handed it to her without saying anything else. She liked it when they cut straight to the chase and she didn't have to pretend to court them. She took the money and put it into her purse before walking around to the passenger side of the car.

"Where we doing this?" she asked, pulling down the bottom of her short dress as she got comfortable in the seat.

"I have a room for a couple of hours."

Overkill, but she liked that he was prepared. She hoped he understood that what he'd paid her wasn't going to get him much more than a handjob, and he could've spent the rest of the money he'd put into the room to get full service from her.

She heard something moving behind her. As the car started rolling forward, she turned around to see another man in the backseat.

"He gonna watch?" she asked, daring him to suggest that he'd given her enough money for the both of them.

The driver made a noise in his throat like he didn't know what she meant, and then looked into the rearview at his friend.

"Oh, yeah. Yeah. He's shy."

People were so weird sometimes. She shrugged as he pulled into the parallel parking space in front of the brothel. It was an old building – in worse disrepair than The Palace, actually – that stood a narrow five stories tall with only four rooms per floor. It looked like someone had just barely squeezed it into The Strip. Occasionally, some poor sap from out of town rented a room for the night or weekend on the super cheap and

realized when they arrived that this was *not* a four-star establishment...
but it mostly was rented out by the hour for the game or a safe-ish place
to get high.

She made eye contact with Zahid behind the counter as he flipped
through a Southern-cooking magazine. He tapped his fingers against his
brow and then at her, acknowledging that he saw her and the two men
she came in with. He was here to make money, just like everyone else with
their fingers in the pot, but he had a baseball bat under the counter and
had run off more than one john who got rough. Zahid didn't play.

They entered a room on the second floor, and the man who had been
driving locked the door behind them. He had a bag with him, and he
was already opening it when Tansi seated herself on the edge of the dingy
sheets that covered the bed.

"I'm feeling generous," She said, taking her purse off of her shoulder
and laying it on the floor beside her. "I'll give you a blowjob for the price
of a ha—"

She stopped short when she looked up and the driver was holding a
girthy strap-on in his hand.

Tansi was rarely surprised.

"Okay," she finally said, leaning back on both hands as they sank into
the mattress. "Sounds like we need to discuss some expectations. What
exactly can I do for you?"

"I want you to fuck him," the driver said, motioning to the shy friend
who was staring at the floor.

"Does Shy Guy want me to fuck him, though?" She asked slowly, watching the other man's face for any sign of emotion other than
wide-eyed terror.

When she got no response, she forced a smile. "You know, this is a little weird for me, and that's saying a lot. I think I'll just give you a refund and head back down..."

"I do," Shy Guy finally blurted out. "I do, please."

Somehow, with the consent, it was now even more weird.

Tansi took a deep breath. "Okay. Nothing goes in me, double the money, and I'll do it."

The driver reached hurriedly into his pocket, counting out smaller bills until he had the correct amount and then pushed it in her direction. She put it into her purse and stood up, unzipping her dress and putting it on the edge of the bed before she took the strap-on and fastened it around her hips. The silicone toy attached to the strap-on was almost comically large.

As the two men took off their clothes, stumbling around the room in a ridiculous clumsy fashion while struggling to get their pants off of their ankles with shaking hands, she hefted the pseudo-dick in her hands.

Shy Guy climbed onto all fours, and the driver retrieved pillows for Tansi's knees. She kind of felt a little flattered that he considered her comfort, although it might have been to add some height to her too, she imagined.

She put one hand against Shy Guy's left asscheek, pulling it to the side. "Got any lube for our friend? If not, I have some in my purse."

The driver came over to her and leaned down, spitting an impressive wad of saliva with equally impressive precision directly onto the tip of the toy. She could feel Shy Guy shaking, and she wondered if it was fear or excitement.

It had been a long time since she'd worn a strap, but she wouldn't mind this over her usual. Somehow, this seemed more fun. Shy Guy took his friend into his mouth, and Tansi pressed into him slowly, still hesitant with the girth of the dildo. The two men were awkwardly silent, so Tansi took their lead.

Normally, the sounds of sex didn't affect her in any way. She was used to all of them: both expected and unexpected. Maybe it was because she felt less dissociated than usual, or maybe it was because she wasn't going somewhere else in her head... but she had to stifle her laughter when she associated the sounds that filled the otherwise silent room with that of an overweight beach dad running down a boardwalk in flip flops.

FIVE

"FUCKING WEIRDOS," TANSI WHISPERED, laughing as she dropped her tits back into her dress. The car burned rubber to drive away, the echoes squealing in the night. Shy Guy ended up tipping her, and they awkwardly gave her a silent car ride back to the Strip. Weird guys, but nice guys.

She pulled a joint out of her jacket pocket and lit it up as she settled against the wall between the bar and club back on The Strip.

The interior of Flaming-O bustled with people, warmth, laughter. Pink Panther had a pulse: the steady beat of music from within that made the glass shake in the barred windows. A massive bouncer stood outside, checking his list like a trashy, bald Santa.

She finished the joint and stamped out the butt, turning to enter the Flaming-O. Someone at the door checked her ID, but there was no cover charge. They patted her down with gentle, polite hands. The Flaming-O just felt safe, somehow. There was no pressure, and she felt invisible, just blending into the crowd of bodies as she made her way to the bar.

Someone was reciting a poem or something on stage: a nervous girl with numerous facial piercings and short, curved bangs over her carefully drawn eyebrows.

The bartender came over to Tansi, and she smiled. "Double Crown, on the rocks."

They had her drink made and in front of her before she could get her purse off of her shoulder. The ice was shaped in perfect, small spheres. It was the little things like the shape of those ice cubes that brought her a glimmer of joy. She paid in cash and sipped the drink as an unofficial announcer came onto the stage.

"That was Gwen Portman. Let's give her a hand for that stellar performance. Next up, we have Elijah Reilly with spoken word."

The announcer sat down at the back of the stage, but no one approached the mic. Tansi shifted in her seat as she looked over her shoulder at the stage. She cringed at the bartender, who shrugged at her. She supposed sometimes they had some no shows, or people who chickened out due to stage fright.

Then she heard a door open.

He entered from the left side of the stage in a plume of coniferous smoke. Tansi could smell it from the corner of the bar where she sat. The exit door slammed shut with a clang, and the man dragged his feet as he shuffled out of the shadows and into the warm glow of the spotlight.

He looked like he needed his hair combed out, but despite the apparent bedhead, he had the darkest circles under his green eyes. He ran his fingers through his hair, knuckles snagging in tangles that he had to shake free from as he leaned forward towards the microphone, voice coming only after a gentle puff of breath.

"Sorry I'm late, but this is how I plan to arrive to every appointment, even death: late, high, and burdened."

No one in the crowd reacted, even as his eyes scanned the dark figures before him, squinting against the light. Tansi was intrigued, and she grabbed her drink from the counter, holding it in both hands before she leaned backwards against the bartop to view the man straight on.

He cleared his throat, furrowing his brow like he was having a conversation, not putting on a performance.

"When's the last time you felt like you mattered? Because I can't remember. Before I was ever born, I knew I wanted to die. Somehow, in the womb, I wound the cord around my neck twice, causing a great compression. A noose, double knotted for durability, because I knew... but they didn't give me a choice.

"We tell our kids the world's cold, but we won't give them a fucking coat. Feel that chill? Dad would say, 'I lost my fingers when I was kid, it'll make you tough. I lost my toes...' along with all of his compassion, I guess. 'We don't want to spoil you with gloves,' Mom said, love necrotic and unrecognizable as a sign of affection anymore.

"So I just keep trying to catch up to the dead man in the mirror, because I never asked to be here, and he's who I want to be when I grow up. But then, sometimes, I notice how blue the sky is and that people are beautiful and I'm thankful that life didn't let me go at seventeen, or twenty-six, or thirty-two, even though I gave it my best effort... because I have so much left to see, so much left to do, so much left to give. Even when it hurts *everywhere, everywhere.*

"They say actions speak louder than words, but this world is so fucking silent. Why do we wait to give eulogies when someone's dead: why do we wait to say the things that matter, do the things that matter, tell people they matter?

"So tell me... do I matter now, or are you going to make me wait?"

There was a profound silence that followed, only disturbed by someone coughing in a corner. Tansi's eyes moved around the room, and then she sat her glass down to clap her cold, wet hands together.

Reluctantly, the room followed suit. The man on the stage seemed surprised, looking directly at her through the haze of white light before the coordinator came back up on stage.

"Thank you for that really... intense performance, as always, Elijah. Next up, we have Cat Malone also doing spoken word."

Tansi didn't hear anything else the person said as she noticed the man approaching her after dismounting the stage. She spun around in her chair, downing the rest of her Crown as she gathered her purse onto her shoulder.

Before she could make an escape, he sidled up to the bar beside her. He sat down casually, leaning on his elbows as he looked over at her through bloodshot eyes.

"Hey," he said, "thanks for that."

She cleared her throat but didn't move. Now it would be too awkward to leave. She would feel weak, scared... but she also didn't want to deal with anyone else tonight. When she didn't respond, she saw him purse his lips together but smile, raising his hand to wave the bartender over. He ordered a Coke.

Just a Coke.

He took a sip through the straw in the glass of fizzy soda and then motioned to her glass. "What are you drinking? Can I get you another one?"

"No," she replied flatly.

"Alright... well, do you come here often? For the show? I don't think I've seen you before."

"I come here pretty often. I don't remember seeing you here before either."

"Yeah, maybe we've just missed each other. Funny how that can happen, isn't it? Just bouncing around in the same space but always on a different trajectory."

"Well, I come here to *avoid* getting hit on by men. So you could say my *trajectory* is intentionally opposite yours."

He shrugged and nodded. "That's fair."

He took another long drink of the soda until air popped in the empty glass beneath the ice.

"Well, I won't harass you. Just wanted to say thanks; hope you enjoyed the performance. I'll be here again this weekend. Eight o'clock."

He got to his feet and pinned a tip under his glass. The bartender had only given him the drink with no other service. The generosity both surprised and, honestly, kind of impressed her. Little kindnesses like this were rare for her to witness.

Tansi spoke quickly, before he could walk away: "So eight fifteen, then?"

He looked up at her and although he didn't say anything, his eyes seemed to somehow dance.

"Since you're always late," she explained, but he was already smiling at her. She thought she felt her face flush.

"Yeah, you got it. Late... but I *will* be here. Maybe I'll see you then."

She shrugged one shoulder and lifted her drink to sip.

He backed away from her for several steps before he turned to leave, disappearing into the crowd.

Tansi's face hurt from resisting the smile that kept tugging at her lips.

Six

Tansi stood at the corner with her arm laced through Alice's, eating the candy bar that the lady from the outreach program had given her. It was good chocolate, a kind she'd never heard of with cursive writing on the label, and it melted quickly against her tongue. It was a sort of fluffy mousse that had just the right amount of sweetness.

"You seen Lucy today?" Tansi asked her.

Alice shook her head. "Nah, I haven't seen her in what feels like a couple of days, at least. You know how she is."

Lucy didn't officially live with them. Tansi actually wasn't sure *where* Lucy lived most of the time. She came and went as she pleased. She had her own key and knew she was welcome at any time. At one point, Tansi thought the girl had crashed with several other young people in a trap house down the way — that was what she had always heard. Now that she was supposedly clean, Tansi figured she had found new digs to avoid the itch. That is, if she really was clean to begin with.

"So... I met this guy a couple of nights ago," Tansi started, voice adopting a strange pitch and cadence that she didn't intend. She finished the last bite of the chocolate bar and let the wrapper fall to the pavement and tumble down the street.

Alice looked at her out of the corner of her eye and then started nervously digging around in her purse. She finally pulled out a blunt.

Tansi could tell she was short on money by the diminishing size of every joint that she had smoked recently. She must have been on a bender.

"Well," Alice said, with the cigarette stuck between her teeth, flicking the lighter with her thin fingers. "I hope you met a bunch of guys a couple of nights ago. Quota's due in a few days and rent in a few weeks, you know."

"You know I'm never late on rent – or quota, for that matter. I make enough to cover me and sometimes you too."

Alice didn't even react to the jab at her. Tansi didn't like to put her willingness to contribute in Alice's face, but sometimes she felt the need to remind her that she *was* valuable. Not to mention that any time Tansi had something to say about doing *anything* other than work, Alice brought up quota and rent. Tansi wondered what she did before she had her to split the rent with.

"So, the guy..." Alice said, disappearing briefly into a cloud of fuschia-lit smoke that smelled faintly of diesel fuel.

"I met him at the Flamingo."

"A gay guy?"

"No... I don't think so. I think he liked me." Tansi felt a stitch of embarrassment in her gut. The admission felt juvenile. They lived in a world where guys didn't like anyone: not in that pure way, not in the way that you grew up fantasizing about it. Men liked satisfaction, no matter how brief. When you weren't easy and you weren't providing them with some kind of pleasure, you were disposable.

"He pay you good?"

"No, I didn't turn him or nothing. We just talked at the bar. I watched him perform, and he was actually really good."

"Perform what? Drag? Music?"

"Spoken word."

"The fuck is spoken word? Aren't all words spoken?"

"It's kind of like reciting a story or poem or something out loud I guess. He offered to buy me a drink, told me to come back and see him perform again tomorrow... I think I might try. He seems different, you know? Like a nice guy."

"...like a weird guy. That's the kind of guy who cuts you up into pieces and puts little ice cubes made out of you in all the neighbors' sweet tea."

"Alright." Tansi sighed.

Alice gave her another side-eye. "What's his name?"

His name? Fuck, what had his name been? Something so average, so normal. Had he told her his name? She could vaguely remember hearing it, somewhere.

"You don't know his name?"

"I can't remember."

"Well, you go see him again... and this time, get his fucking name, won't you? Maybe a phone number?"

Tansi felt relieved by her response, and they exchanged soft, understanding smiles.

A black car pulled up slowly, interrupting them. The windows were tinted so dark, it had to be illegal. The exterior of the car looked freshly waxed, glistening like a dark mirror in the night. A car like that screamed money, and both Alice and Tansi were fully attentive.

The interior of the car was too dark to see inside, but a hand extended from the shadows and into the night. The fingers were long and slim, tipped by sharp, dark nails.

It was a woman.

Female clients weren't very common. They weren't unheard of, but Tansi wasn't even sure she'd seen one in person. She'd been involved in a couple of threesomes, had a few non-transactional encounters, but never a woman checking out the girls taking a stroll.

Tansi looked over at Alice, ready to give her first dibs. Honestly, she was a little intimidated.

Alice looked the car over end to end and then said, "Nah. She's yours."

Tansi walked over to the car, leaning into the window. The car smelled like new leather; the interior was solid black, spotless and clean. She was surprised by the woman sitting in the driver's seat, wearing a dress that was black just like Tansi's, except – she was sure – it had ten times the price on the tag.

And she was hot as fuck.

It wasn't like Tansi never had a good-looking john, but this girl could likely have anyone she wanted, which made Tansi wonder what the catch would be.

"Hey, baby," Tansi said with a smile. "What can I do you for?"

"Just oral. I have a room at a hotel," the woman responded. Her voice was just an octave lower than Tansi expected, but rich and smooth. Her eyes were a dark hazel: such a deep brown that they were nearly black, with flecks of green and yellow. The pink light from the streets gave those eyes a slick, animal-like sheen: a silvered, oily gloss.

"Where's the hotel?" Tansi asked, already pursing her lips together to apologize.

"Uptown."

"I don't usually go that far with first-time clients. How about we see how we get along tonight, and you can come visit me again, huh?"

The woman's hand curled around the steering wheel, fingertips tracing the curve as she considered.

"We can park in the alleyway a few blocks up. The stores are closed. Very discreet. I'll just charge you fifty."

"Get in."

"Yes, ma'am," Tansi responded with a grin, walking briskly in front of the car to circle around to the passenger seat. She felt so small inside the car. The ceiling towered over her head and there was so much leg room that she didn't expect. The backseat of the sedan was even roomier. She couldn't get over how new the car looked. No one kept their car this clean.

The woman didn't speak as she pulled down the street at Tansi's direction, steering the dark car into a dark alleyway immune to any light from The Strip.

She put the car into park, leaving the quiet, 80's synthpop on the radio as she exited the vehicle and climbed into the back. For a brief moment Tansi was bathed in the brilliance of the dome light, shattering some of the illusion of mystery and intrigue that the woman had carried. She sat in the back of the car in her black dress, hair falling over her shoulders in a chestnut cascade. In only another moment, they were bedecked in darkness and the woman was something inhuman once more.

She hadn't paid Tansi yet, and that was something she *always* made sure happened. If you didn't get payment up front, you risked not getting paid at all. Tansi turned around the passenger seat to face the woman as she sat in the center of the seat, leaning towards her.

"Can I kiss you?"

Tansi returned the smile. "That's not usually part of it, hon."

The woman shrugged and sat back, and Tansi got onto her knees, leaning over the center console as she ran her fingers up the client's thigh. She traced the curve of her leg up to her hip, fingers searching for her underwear but finding that she wasn't wearing any. She danced along her lower stomach, feeling the sensitive skin twitch beneath her touch as she dipped down and traveled between her legs. She slipped two fingers inside her and circled gently with her thumb.

The woman put one leg on either front seat and Tansi pulled her hand back to wink at her and suck her fingers before descending between her legs again, this time with her mouth. She edged her tongue along the silky, slick flesh; saliva pooled beneath her tongue.

As she worked, she heard the woman speak, voice sounding distant and muffled as her thighs gently pressed the sides of Tansi's head.

"I killed a man."

Tansi hesitated for a moment, huffing hot air against the equal warmth of the woman's body. She felt her hand wind into her hair, applying gentle pressure and she resumed reluctantly.

"I've killed a lot of men, but I've never told anyone. I needed to tell someone. I wanted someone to..." Her breath hitched and her body tensed. "It always feels— God, it feels *so good* to watch them die."

Tansi had heard a lot of clients say a lot of things to help themselves get off. There was one guy who sang *I'm a Little Teapot* every damn time as he climaxed. He had a heart attack at home and died. She saw it on the news. It was the first time she heard that he had been an elementary school teacher and a father of four.

This was one of the weirder things, though. Maybe this girl was a freak, liked horror movies, that kind of thing. Some girls were into some fucked-up dark romance books; Lucy went through that phase. Shapeshifters with dog cocks and shit. Whatever got you off, she supposed. She could play along.

She put a small whine into her voice and gently bit into the woman's thigh. "Tell me more."

The woman's hand tightened at the feeling of her teeth, and she pressed into Tansi's mouth when she returned to her.

"I drugged him. Cut him— open. I buried my hands inside him."

"He deserved it," Tansi panted, putting on the best show she could with her voice.

"They all do," the woman responded quietly.

"Did he scream?"

"Yes."

"Did you like it?" Drawing what flesh she could into her mouth, she gently sucked and swirled her tongue around it.

"*Fuck yes.*" The woman's voice was barely audible as she tensed, quivering beneath her touch. Tansi slid her tongue up once in a last long, pressured swipe as the woman's body relaxed all at once. She let out a shuddering breath, and her hand released Tansi's hair.

Tansi returned to her seat a little too quickly, reaching back to fix the wad of frizzled hair and adjust her dress. The woman wasted no time either, putting her feet onto the floorboard and pulling her dress down. She grabbed her purse from the front console and walked to Tansi's side of the car.

She looked up at the woman as she opened the door, seemingly ready to kick her out already. Maybe she was disappointed in her service. She had gone from a puddle in the backseat to composed in an instant, maybe even annoyed. Tansi couldn't really get a read on her expression. It was just... cold.

Tansi smiled at her, retrieving her own purse and putting it onto her shoulder as she exited.

She cleared her throat, "That'll be fifty, doll."

The woman pulled bills out of her purse and handed them to Tansi, maintaining an unsettling eye contact as Tansi realized she was handing her two one hundred dollar bills.

"You... sure?" she asked.

"Can I walk you back?"

"Okay," Tansi responded awkwardly, and the pair left the alleyway together.

The first few steps were silent, other than the sound of their heels on the pavement. Tansi kept her eye on the part of the street she strolled, finding that her hands were shaking in nervousness. She didn't like this.

"My name's Missy," the woman said, voice flat.

Missy was more of a street name than Tansi was, she thought, but she didn't say anything. She just gave her the *that's nice* smile that you give a kid who announced they'd shit their pants.

A man stumbled out of Pink Panther ahead of them, stumbling four steps at a time down the street with a glass still in his hand. No one bothered to try and stop him, apparently they didn't need the cup badly enough to ask him to come back inside. He immediately had his eyes on the women.

Tansi sidestepped to give the man a wide berth, avoiding any contact with him, either direct or indirect. She wasn't in the mood to entertain a drunk dumbass like him.

"Hey, don't be shy," he slurred at her, turning back to watch as she moved closer to the wall of the nearest building. Not looking forward, he slammed into Missy, nearly toppling her over. He dropped his glass and it shattered on the sidewalk, splattering what was left of his alcohol on their calves.

"Aw, shit," he chuffed.

He noticed Missy for the first time then, looking her up and down before reaching out with a confident hand to grab a handful of her ass. Tansi's blood boiled, not for Missy specifically, but at the *audacity*.

"How about you, huh? You want to go have some fun?"

Missy smiled, the corners of her dark-painted lips curling. "I'm parked just up here. I'll drive us to my place."

"Now we're—" he hiccuped, "—talking."

She slung her arm around his torso, supporting all of his sloppy weight as she looked back over her shoulder at Tansi and winked.

"When in Rome."

Missy was good at faking emotion, but she struggled to mask her disgust as the drunkard hung off of her. He reeked of cheap cologne, booze, and sex: the staples of the strip club. He breathed all over her, breath hot and offensive. He was dead weight, barely moving his legs as she struggled to drag him into the alleyway.

She had only been in town a few days, and she had already familiarized herself with all of the good hunting grounds. Jessop Terrace, or "The Strip" as everyone seemed to call it, was a *prime* location. Virtually no police presence, no street surveillance, little traffic, and more dirtbags than she could ever hope for.

"Oh, shoot," she sighed. "Where is my car?"

She let go of him, really hoping he'd just crumple to the ground, but he caught himself and looked down the empty alley.

"That's fine, little lady." He laughed, stumbling into her again, but this time hard enough that he pushed her into the opposing wall. The breath was nearly knocked out of her. The brick scraped her bare shoulders, and he pressed every possible inch of himself against her. "This will be alright, won't it? Just a quickie right here?"

"I don't know." She pretended to whine, turning her face away from him as he placed sloppy kisses on her jawline. It made her skin crawl, but more than that, it really pissed her off.

"Shhh…" he hissed, resting one forearm on the wall behind her and fumbling with the zipper of his pants with the other hand.

"No." She tested him, attempting to push away and out of his grasp. He pushed back, pressing her harder into the wall.

She reached up, grabbing him under the chin with her hand. His eyes widened in surprise at first, and then he laughed.

"Oooh, you like it rough?"

"Maybe," she said, squeezing his cheeks until her long nails dug into his flesh.

She let go to shove him with both hands, knowing that in his inebriated state, he could barely stand, let alone keep his balance. He stumbled away from her and fell into the opposite wall. She was on him in an instant, pressing her body against his like he had done to her.

He was thrilled with it, now using both hands to try to free his attempted hard-on. Alcohol could be such a mood killer sometimes.

He kissed her, pressing until their teeth touched. She bit his lower lip, applying pressure until she tasted a metallic tang on the tip of her tongue. He moaned into her.

"Protection," she whispered, eyes lighting up like she'd just remembered.

She reached into her purse and started digging.

"Oh, you're just… all kinds of prepared aren't you? You dirty little—"

Missy pulled the taser out of her purse and shoved it straight into the exposed, oozing head of his limp dick.

The pop of electricity was louder than the scream that left his lungs. A pair of men walked by on the street, and she tried to imitate sounds of pleasure, leaning into him as she kept the contacts on his flesh.

She felt him stop breathing, frothing at the mouth as he tensed against her. The men hesitated, and she buried her face into his shoulder, moaning. They laughed, giving a thumbs up, and then went on their way.

When they were out of sight, she let go and he fell to the ground, gasping and choking on his own saliva.

"You fucking bitch! What the fuck!" He fell onto his back, reeling from both pain and delirium.

"Oh," She tsk'd, standing straddle-legged over him as he tried to scoot away and get to his feet. "You love our savagery when it suits you. Don't you like it rough, sweetheart? Don't you want to have *fun*?"

She raised her heeled shoe and planted it on the crotch of his unzipped pants before applying all of her weight. The fabric of his pants saved him from the full force, she presumed, but the satisfying crunch of tissue and the screams that followed were enough for her.

Missy pulled a knife from her purse and set the bag on the ground before she dropped to her knees, sitting on his midsection.

"Shhhh. You don't want anyone to interrupt us, do you? Really, though..." She looked over her shoulder at the street behind them. "I think out here... no one cares if you scream. Sing for me, baby."

Missy opened the knife, holding the handle with two hands as she plunged it into his chest. He tried to punch her and she sliced his knuckles open, satisfied at how the flesh peeled away from the bone much like the scrotum did when you squeezed a testicle and slid a blade across it. Peeling nuts was one of her favorite things to do when she had time.

One of his blows landed on her check, leaving a splatter of blood from his torn knuckles and a throbbing pain from the impact.

She pierced one of his lungs, and his voice became more faint, to the point that she could hear the knife grind against his bones on each thrust. He continued to fight her, arms flailing uselessly between them. She cut open his throat. Air hissed from the wound like a party kazoo. Missy wiped the blade of her knife clean on his shirt and laid it to the side. Then she shoved her index finger in his exposed windpipe, occupying the entire space. She left it there, staring into his eyes as he flailed, chest heaving, sucking uselessly against the first joint of her finger as he suffocated.

Seven

"I didn't know you were that good at eating pussy," Alice said, fixing her short hair in the mirror.

Tansi leaned forward, drawing the pink lipstick across her top lip. It was in a gold vial and had the faintest fragrance to it; she couldn't remember where she'd gotten it, but it had become one of her favorite shades. Most men liked red, she'd noticed, but no one was going to bitch about the color of your lips at the end of the day.

"I'm not," she insisted.

"Well, you probably didn't get paid for your personality."

Alice snickered, and Tansi jabbed her with her elbow.

"She was *really* weird though. She had a fantasy about killing men, I think."

"I like her already."

"Really, though… I got a weird vibe. She kind of scared me a little, just seemed like she was missing a few screws."

"We get that type a lot."

"Yeah, maybe. Listen, there's something else I want to talk to you about."

Alice paused her makeup application and looked over at Tansi, one eye darkened with liner and the other naked and pale.

"What?"

Tansi moved to sit on the closed toilet lid and sighed. "I talked to that lady, you know. The one that drives around and hands out shit."

"Miss Ferrari?"

"Yeah, whatever. Her."

"What are you talking to her for?"

"I asked if she could help Lucy. You know... get out of here."

Alice paused another moment before dropping the eyeliner pen back into her bag.

"And what did she say?"

"She said she'd do all she could if Lucy would accept the help."

"If I'd accept help for what?"

Both women looked up to see Lucy standing in the doorway of the bathroom. She looked tired. Her face seemed a little puffy and swollen.

"Hey, Luce," Tansi said with a subtle smile, "I was going to talk to you about this... I just wanted to run it by Alice first."

"Well, you've run it by her, and I'm here now." She crossed her arms over her chest, jaw set. "So what is it?"

"You know that Miss Fer—Ferrarese, right?"

"I've seen her, yeah. Took one of her goodie bags a time or two."

"I talked to her about helping you get out of the life, if you want to. She said she'd help you out if you'd let her."

"I don't need help. My man's going to take care of everything. I told him about the baby yesterday." She uncrossed her arms to nervously pick at her fingernails. "He was surprised, said he needed a little time to think about everything, but he'd take care of it. He's a good guy."

"Who is he?" Tansi asked, her gut tied in tight knots.

Lucy didn't respond, leaning against the doorway as she averted her eyes to the ceiling like a child who didn't want to admit they were wrong.

"Tell us who he is, Lucy," Alice demanded.

"Aaron."

Everyone fell silent.

Aaron was DJ's cousin. He pushed a lot of drugs and sometimes worked as security at Pink Panther. He wasn't as bad as DJ, but he was torn from the same cloth. More dangerous than his family relation, though, was his desire to impress and please DJ. The girls sometimes joked and called him AJ because he could've come straight out of DJ's asshole.

If DJ found out that Aaron had been sleeping around with his girls and had knocked one of them up, he would be pissed.

"Lucy, this is bad," Alice pressed, but her voice was pleading and quiet.

"No, no." Lucy laughed, tears brimming her eyes as she came into the small bathroom. She stood in front of Alice, cupping their hands together. "It's all going to be okay. Aaron knows DJ would be pissed if he knew... I trust him. He said to give him a few days to figure out what he needs to do."

Tansi was glad she was sitting down, because she didn't know what to do with herself. She started chewing her fingernail. She spoke around her clenched teeth, little clicks and pops of the nail severing between her incisors.

"I don't want to overstep, Luce. But me and Alice just care about you. Will you please talk to that lady? Even if AJ is going to get out of here and settle down or whatever... she can make sure you *and the baby* are safe until then. That's what you want, right?"

Lucy backed away from them, for a moment just staring ahead. When she took a shuddering breath, it was as though she sucked all of the oxygen out of the room, and suddenly Tansi felt very claustrophobic.

"Alright. I'll talk to her," Lucy said, voice low and quiet.

"No commitment to nothing," Alice confirmed supportively. "If anything, Aaron should be excited that you'll get some free medical care on fEmpower's dime."

"So you'll call her tomorrow, then?"

"Do you one better, Tans. I'll call her tonight."

Lucy turned and walked out of the bathroom; Alice and Tansi exchanged glances that were both relieved and concerned.

"She'll be fine now."

"I'm not so sure. DJ won't let this slide."

"If we can get her out of here, I don't care what DJ does to Aaron. Fuck him."

Tansi didn't argue but instead got to her feet and tugged the bottom of her crop top before checking herself in the mirror again. She reached down for a cell phone and noted the time, finding it later than she had hoped.

"I'm gonna go out. I'll be back."

Alice dropped her lipstick in her makeup bag. "Hold up and I'll just walk with you."

"I'm not gonna work right now. It'll be later. I'm just gonna go chill for a while, you know?"

Alice looked at her in both eyes and then up and down. "Don't forget we got the quota plus rent coming due."

"I made enough off that girl to earn a few hours to myself, don't you think?"

"I think you're fucking stupid if you think people like us are *ever* ahead."

Tansi shrugged her shoulders, turning her chin up as she walked out of the bathroom. She could already hear Lucy on the phone and, out of the corner of her eye, saw her sitting cross legged on the bed. Lucy always had strong emotions, and Tansi was satisfied to see what might have been excitement on her face. This would be good for her. Sometimes things really did work out.

Tansi crossed the street, trying not to make eye contact with anyone who was driving by or walking to Pink Panther. She made a beeline for the Flaming-O, pushing her way through the front door and flashing her ID in one movement. The guy at the door, a burly bear of a man, nodded at her without even looking. She wondered if he recognized her. The moment she was fully inside the bar, she felt a sense of calm wash over her. There was something about the Flaming-O that was just cleaner, more welcoming, and less dangerous feeling than any other place on The Strip. Somehow, even the apartment felt like being in a cardboard box in a war zone.

There were more people inside today than there had been the last time she was here. A man with an acoustic guitar sat on stage with his knees bent up, feet propped on the upper rung of the stool. It made him look like a folksy grasshopper as he leaned into the microphone and sang with his eyes closed, fingers strumming from memory.

She tried not to make it obvious that she was looking for the guy, scanning the crowd as she zigzagged to the bar. She sat down, laying her purse on the bartop as she looked over her shoulder one more time.

The bartender came over to her, the same one that waited on her last time. They smiled.

"Crown on the rocks?"

"Double, please," she responded, looking around again as they prepared her drink with those perfect little cubes.

The drink being slid across the bartop got her attention, and she turned around to thank the bartender quietly as she slid cash across to them.

They took the money but waited. "Are you looking for Reilly?"

Elijah Reilly. That was it.

"No," Tansi responded, "I'm just looking."

"He finished his set earlier, about an hour ago, but he's probably out back smoking. He hangs around."

"Good to know," she said, trying to sound disinterested.

"I could text him," they offered, picking their cell phone up from beneath the counter.

"No. No, no. That's fine. Actually... I have to go. I— think I left my stove on," Tansi said, face flushing. She got to her feet, turning the drink up until the sweating cubes moistened the tip of her nose. "Thank you so much. See you again soon."

"You just got here?" The bartender seemed confused but raised their hand awkwardly as Tansi retreated through the crowd and back into the street.

She took a deep breath of the dense, polluted air, turning her eyes up to the artificial-pink atmosphere above her. Her heart was pounding, and she released the air between her lips as she willed it to still.

This was ridiculous... but she loved the way she felt like the child she had been not so long ago.

Eight

It never really felt like night on Jessop Terrace. Every day felt like just another *really long* day. The sun sat, replaced in small increments by the man-made glow of the street lights. It transformed a dingy, quiet street where you locked your doors into a street alive with the temptation and promise of debauchery and indulgence.

This was Sin City, and she didn't sleep.

It was nearing two in the morning when Tansi's client dropped her off at The Strip, handing her a couple of bucks with his sticky fingers, dirty nails brushing against her palm as she took the wadded bills and shoved them into her purse in their still-faceted state.

She moved to the nearest street lamp, leaning against it as she tugged the back of her dress down, trying to cover the tear in her stockings. She could feel the soft flesh in the separation of coarse netting.

A truck rolled down the street, engine rumbling with such a deep growl that she felt it in her chest. She stiffened at the sight of it coming towards her. It was DJ's truck; she would recognize it anywhere. She tucked her hair behind her ear, preparing to head down the street in the opposite direction so maybe he wouldn't stop her.

The truck kept time beside her, and without looking, she heard the window roll down.

"Hey, Tansi," DJ said, voice taking on a playful tone.

Tansi stopped, trying to look like she was surprised it was him. He stopped the truck alongside the sidewalk, and she wandered over to the window, forcing a smile.

"Hey, DJ. Something wrong? Not like you to be driving around out here."

"Funny thing, having to do a little work on the ground myself. Sometimes you have to make sure shit is done right, you know?"

"Yeah, I know."

"You got anything you think I need to know? Getting real tired of people thinking they can keep secrets."

Tansi swallowed. "No."

"No?"

"Nothing I can think of."

"Get in."

"I got a lot to do, DJ. Running short tonight."

He enunciated every word with a sharpness. "Get in the truck, Tansi."

She hesitated, and he noticed. She watched his knuckles pale as he squeezed the steering wheel, and she walked over to the door, popping it open and climbing into the elevated seat. He spun his tires as he took off, vehicle clanging against loose grates on the road as Tansi struggled to buckle herself in.

"Heya, Tans."

A voice from the backseat of the extended cab raised the hair along the back of her neck. She turned slowly, only giving one eye the view of the two men who sat in the seat behind her. The one who spoke was Donnie: that weasel-faced, rodent of a man that owned Pink Panther. He wore a white button-up with an open suit jacket and a pair of slacks. The rings on his fingers were obnoxiously large, clicking together as he rapped his fingertips on his knee.

Beside him, directly behind Tansi, was Aaron.

Her instincts told her to open the truck door and dive out. She might as well be a mouse sitting between three sadistic cats, and risking getting hit by a car seemed like the better life decision. Instead, she turned back towards the road, sitting up straighter and feigning confidence. DJ was pulling down a side street off of Jessop Terrace, one of those roads that glowed with a certain jaundice of yellow lights. It seemed surreal, sickly, compared to the pink of The Strip.

The truck coasted down the street before turning into an alleyway beside a seedy bar. She recognized the place. She knew it was the bar where DJ took clients when he didn't want Donnie in his business, almost like a safe zone for more intimate work... but Donnie was here now.

"What are we doing out here?" Tansi asked, pleased with how even and calm her voice sounded. "You gonna kill me?"

The three men laughed, voices echoing in the cab like the barking of dogs.

As suddenly as it had started, it stopped, and DJ reached over to grab her chin, turning it towards him.

"You done something worth getting killed over?"

"Of course not," she said, voice quiet.

Tansi forced herself to look him in the eyes. She wished he would just tell her what was wrong, what it was that he was looking for. Her mind reeled as she sought any reason that he may have had to be mad at her, to blame her for anything. She had always laid low, though, always did as she was told, always paid on time.

He let go of her face, but somehow aggressively, slinging her head to the side so forcefully that she heard her neck pop at the base of her skull.

"You know, I do a lot for the family, don't I? You girls mean the world to me. I make sure you aren't bothered by nobody, I make sure you have plenty of work, and trust me, I take way less money than any other guy in the business. Don't I, Donnie?"

Donnie leaned in, nodding his head as though he were explaining something to a child. "Very generous man DJ is. You got it *good*."

DJ continued, "So when I hear that somebody is betraying and taking advantage of my good nature, I get a little upset. I lose my temper just a little."

This time he looked for support and confirmation from Aaron, turning to look in the back seat. "Right, AJ?"

Aaron leaned forward between the seats like Donnie had, and Tansi noticed that his left eye was purple and bulging so much that it was swollen shut. A small bandage held a piece of spliced brow together, and he had a fresh scab of blood on his lip.

"You see what I mean, don't you?" DJ asked. "I don't want to hurt you, Tansi. So I'm going to ask you a few questions, and if I'm satisfied with your answers, I'll just let you go back to work. How about that? Easy enough to tell the truth, isn't it?"

"I don't got nothing to hide from you, Deej," Tansi responded, infuriated at how afraid she was. Her voice shook, and she felt like the vibration started inside and worked its way out. She leaned back into the seat, staring forward at the dark alley that stretched before them. DJ didn't make her look back at him, so she just listened instead.

"Do you know where Lucy is?"

The question took Tansi by surprise.

"Lucy? No, I—"

"Wrong answer," DJ said, with a smile that disappeared as quickly as it appeared.

Before Tansi realized what was happening, Aaron reached across the seat, pulling something tight against Tansi's throat. A scream choked out of her as her head and neck were pinned against the headrest. She reached up, grappling for the thing around her throat as spots burst in her vision like ink droplets in water.

It felt like a belt, something an inch or two wide. She could feel Aaron's breath on her ear and the squeak of his hands as he wound the leather around his palms.

"Alright, let's give her another shot," DJ said, voice calm.

The tension against her throat slackened, and she could pull more air into her lungs. Her chest ached, burning with the desire for oxygen.

"I know Lucy has been staying with you. Alice told me. Do you understand? Just nod."

Tansi nodded slowly, head throbbing with stress.

"We waited outside for her yesterday, and she wasn't there. She also wasn't at the crack house she used to stay at. In fact... nobody has seen her recently. Donnie's got tabs everywhere, you know. So I'm going to ask you again... do you know where she is? Before you answer, I want you to think about what you're going to say first."

Tansi accepted the opportunity. She took several deep, shaky breaths through her nose, tears pouring down her flushed cheeks. They had already talked to Alice, and she had told them that Lucy stayed with them sometimes. What else had she told them?

She hated herself for what she admitted next.

"She stays with us sometimes, but she comes and goes. We never know when she will be there. Last I heard, she had gone talking to that nosy bitch from the crisis center. I think she went with her. She's probably long gone by now; they've probably got her in a program or shelter or something."

She hoped that was true. She hoped that Lucy was as far away from here as possible and that she wasn't coming back. She knew better, though... because Aaron was in the backseat.

"That's a good girl. See? Alice already told me everything. I just wanted to see if I could trust you. I need to be able to trust you." He reached over to caress her thigh, and her gut turned sour. There were a lot of terrible men in this business, in this city, in this world, but DJ's very soul was filthy.

"Alright, so there's nothing I can do about where she goes or what she does. I told you the truth, what else do you want from me?"

"I don't need you to do anything. I just needed to remind you who is in charge around here. Everybody is going to remember it from now on." He shot a sharp glare at Aaron in the backseat. "Everybody."

"I've never done you dirty, Deej," Tansi insisted, leaning forward as Aaron released the belt around her throat, pulling it into the backseat with a zip and then pop that caused her to flinch.

DJ didn't respond. He put the truck in reverse and backed out of the alleyway.

NINE

TANSI PURPOSEFULLY STAYED AT the apartment only while Alice was working. She hadn't talked to her in a few days, not since the encounter with DJ. Alice knew something was going on, but judging by the way she didn't pry, Tansi assumed she had figured it out. Giving someone the cold shoulder when you lived with and shared a bed with them was hard. Tansi had taken to sleeping on the couch when her back could handle it. The cushions were so worn and thin that she could feel the frame through them when she lay there.

She was making less money since she was waiting for Alice to finish up before she went down, but she was still scraping up enough to pay DJ what he needed. Rent was going to be tight, and she wasn't sure she'd have enough to help buy groceries.

She sat on the table by the window, staring out at the vibrant street below. The lights left jagged, shiny pink scars across the wet pavement. She wanted to go back to the Flaming-O and maybe see Elijah Reilly again. It felt silly that she still thought about him after only meeting him a single time. Right now, she didn't have the money to justify going in. She could get in for free and sit on the bar, but it felt wrong to not buy a drink even if it was just a placeholder for her.

Her cell phone buzzed, and she put her feet down just long enough to give herself leverage to reach it on the edge of the couch before she settled down by the window.

It was Alice.

Tansi paused, wondering if she should answer or send it straight to voicemail. She looked out the window again and saw Alice standing on the corner, looking up at the window as she held the phone to her ear. A black car had parked by the sidewalk in front of her.

She answered, "Yeah."

"Client is down here requesting you," Alice said.

"Tell him I'm not working right now. It'll be later."

"It isn't a guy. It's that girl from the other night."

"Well, fuck, tell her I'll be *right* down," Tansi responded, getting up and stumbling around the room. She grabbed a tube top, tights, and a pair of shorts.

"Tansi?" Alice's voice still came from the other side.

"What?"

"I don't want you to be mad at me. I can't stand it. I know this is about DJ, and I just want you to know I didn't tell him anything he didn't already know. He was testing me. Aaron had told him about Lucy and the baby. He already knew."

Tansi clenched her teeth and sighed, moving into the bathroom to fine tune her eye makeup and reapply her pink lipstick.

"I know. He did the same thing to me. It's okay. Let's just hope Lucy knows what's good for her and stays away."

"She'll be back. You know how stubborn she is. She'll be back for Aaron."

Tansi didn't let her say more and ended the call, tucking the phone into her purse as she headed out the door.

The static hiss of tires through water filled the night air: like thousands of pieces of paper being torn down the middle. Tansi crossed the road carefully, heels adding a staccato to the harsh ambience of the rainy street.

Alice moved away as Tansi approached, giving her space but keeping an eye on the interaction between her and the client. Tansi leaned over by the window, and the woman inside looked back at her without the smallest sign of interest or desire.

Her dark eyes still looked matte, the sort of dead-eyed stare that betrayed no emotion. Tonight, she wore a pair of jeans and a low-cut shirt beneath a denim jacket. Her hair hung down around her shoulders, lips painted the deepest black.

Tansi had opened her mouth to offer a greeting, but the woman cut her off. "Will you come with me tonight?"

Her voice was so level and cold. It lacked any kind of variation of tone or vibrance of personality. Tansi just couldn't put her finger on it, but she had a chilled feeling in the most primitive part of her brain – an ice-cold prickling of sensation that pressed her towards caution.

She didn't show any of that as she leaned down into the open window, smiling as coyly as she could manage, "Well, if I'm out with you, I'm not making any money here. So if I go, it'll have to be worthwhile."

The woman wasn't impressed, her eyes moving across every inch of Tansi's face. It wasn't a look full of desire or longing; it was a calculating evaluation, tinged with annoyance and impatience.

"I gave you four times what you asked for last time," she said. "I think you know this will be worth your while."

"Let me just tell my roommate not to wait up for me. Be right back."

Tansi walked towards Alice, keeping her back to the client's car. Alice was taking a drag from a cigarette, one that looked like it had been partially smoked and then extinguished to save for later.

"Get her plate for me?" Tansi asked quietly.

Alice's eyes drifted to the car behind her briefly, and then she blew a stream of smoke into the air above them. The damp air clung droplets to her wig, adorning her in a crown of perspiration.

"You going somewhere with her?"

"Yeah, could use the extra money."

"You know nobody pays like that unless there's a catch, right?"

"Yeah, probably."

"You know you got no self-preservation at all, right?"

"Get the plate. I'll check in with you."

Alice nodded but didn't say anything else. She never warned Tansi about getting in the car with multiple men, or for turning a trick who was an *obvious* red flag. Yet now she wanted Tansi to turn this down. Despite everything, Tansi *did* trust the other woman's intuition.

That didn't stop her from sliding into the passenger seat. She seated herself, sitting up straight enough that she could see out the rearview mirror for a fraction of a moment, long enough to see Alice lift her phone to take a photo of the back of the car as it pulled down the street.

"So where you staying at, baby?" Tansi asked, settling against the seat as she watched the road ahead of them.

"The Koplin Grand."

Tansi tried not to act surprised when she said it, instead awkwardly tucking hair behind one of her ears, pulling a trapped strand free from her earring. The Koplin Grand was one of the most expensive hotels in the city.

"Do you know it?" the woman asked.

"Hm? Oh, the Grand. Yeah, I know it."

As the black car pulled onto the busy city street, Tansi found herself leaning into the door to gaze through the tinted window. The lights here felt cleaner and brighter, and the buildings somehow cast less shadow. The illumination didn't penetrate the interior of the car, and as they weaved in and out of traffic down the busy city highway, it was as though they were captive in their own little bubble of darkness.

"So you in town for something or...?" Tansi ventured. She didn't know why she asked. She never talked to clients, never wanted to know anything about their lives or families or anything that they did. This was an unusual circumstance, though. An air of mystique surrounded the woman, and Tansi could not resist the intrigue.

The woman didn't answer immediately, wrist draped over the steering wheel. She couldn't have had enough control of the vehicle that way and, honestly, it raised an inkling of concern in Tansi's gut.

In the silence, she added another awkward question. "What did you say your name was again?"

"Missy."

That was right... how could she have forgotten?

"That's an interesting name," Tansi added, leaning away from the window long enough to let the fog from her breath disappear.

"Short for Artemis."

"That's... even more interesting."

Who named their kids such ridiculous names?

"That accent," Missy started. "Where are you from?"

It was Tansi's turn to hesitate. She didn't like sharing information about anything before she joined the life, but what could it hurt? After all, she was prodding into Missy's personal life.

"A little town called Last Bend. It's—"

"I know where Last Bend is. My biological mother was from White-branch." Missy turned the car into the parking lot of The Koplin Grand, bypassing valet services and pulling into the garage. "Small world. I was adopted by a couple out of town, out of state. I stalked my real parents for a little while. I wasn't missing much – boring people. I did have a younger brother, though. He was a little more interesting, but he's dead now. It's a shame because from what I hear, we had a lot in common."

"I'm so sorry. What happened to him?"

Missy smiled, tilting her head to the side so that her dark hair fell away from her face and across her shoulder, "Shootout with a cop, I think."

Before Tansi had an opportunity to respond, Missy put the car in park. Tansi quickly exited, following the percussion of Missy's boots in the otherwise quiet reverb of the garage.

They crossed a quiet side street, the distant sound of a siren howling into the night. It wasn't something she'd heard so close in a long time, and she found herself shaking off a chill. Police rarely ventured out to the strip, and EMTs went even less often. When someone died, it seemed like their body just disappeared without any fanfare. Even in death, they belonged to the street.

The lobby of The Koplin Grand alone was spectacular. Everything was so bright and clean. The glare of it nearly blinded Tansi as she walked through the revolving door behind Missy. She blinked rapidly, using her finger to keep her mascara and eyeliner from running. She realized as she lifted her hand how dingy her flesh looked, so she crossed her arms self-consciously.

She didn't speak as they rode the elevator up twelve floors and then walked down a hall of deep green and silver to the door of room 1215. Tansi noted the room number just in case and entered more slowly than Missy had. She surveyed the room, looking for signs of any extra people that might be waiting for them to get there.

Instead she found the spacious room completely empty. A bathroom was to her left, kitchenette to her right, and straight ahead was the bed and a massive set of floor-length windows that surveyed the entire city.

As Missy sat on the bed to remove her boots, Tansi slowly walked to the windows. Her eyes roved over the twinkling lights of the city, the endless glowing specks of headlights marching up and down the highway. She even saw the faintest tinge of pink, like a wound, where Jessop Terrace was nestled among the illumination of the city. It was rimmed in darkness, a necrosis of closed businesses and undesirable slums on every side.

"I said I'd pay you well... but not to stare out the window." Missy's voice came from behind her, but closer than expected, so Tansi flinched.

She looked over her shoulder to see Missy's set of hazel eyes staring, if not into her very soul, then through her. Tansi dropped her purse directly to the floor, turning to face her with a smile.

"Of course. What do you want— me to go down on you again?"

"I was thinking of a little role reversal."

Tansi had plenty of male clients who got their own personal brand of pleasure by thinking they could get her off. It was often a certain type of man; she could usually spy them a mile away.

Her hesitation worked in her favor. Missy moved away from her and opened the top drawer in the hotel dresser. She reached in and retrieved a worn wallet with a crest or emblem on it. Tansi thought it might say the name of a fraternity, which seemed like a weird choice for the woman who owned it. She removed several bills, fanning them out in her hand.

Tansi tried to hide her surprise, instead taking a slow step over to accept the bills and count them.

"Will that work?"

Would that work... Jesus Christ, *of course* it would work.

She shrugged her shoulders, putting the money on the bedside table as Missy approached her, maintaining that cold eye contact as she unbuttoned Tansi's shorts. Tansi shook her hips enough to let them slide to the floor. She left the thigh high tights on, lying back onto the bed. Missy didn't drop to her knees immediately, as Tansi had expected. Instead, she walked back to the drawer and retrieved something else: a slip-chain collar.

Tansi sat up, concern on her features. This wasn't something they had discussed, and Tansi didn't *trust* this woman. Missy held up the collar before slipping her own head into it.

"Not for you," she said quietly, moving back to the bed as Tansi put her legs onto the mattress, leaning back against the plush pillows.

As she crawled towards her, Tansi couldn't help but feel somehow trapped and vulnerable, a sensation she was not often subjected to. Missy rested on her elbows between Tansi's parted thighs, lifting the end of the chain to her.

"Put your finger in the ring," she instructed.

Tansi obeyed, slipping the ring onto her middle finger reluctantly. It was cold and uncomfortable, pressing its wide girth against her adjacent fingers with an intrusive pressure.

"Choke me."

Tansi was no stranger to this kind of play either, so why was she nervous? She gently drew her hand back, feeling and hearing the pop of each link along the ring against Missy's neck.

"How hard?"

"If you think you're killing me, pull harder."

TEN

MISSY PULLED THE DARK car in front of The Palace and came to a stop against the street. She didn't put the car in park, and it idled quietly there. Tansi had been running her fingers over the places where the chain had pinched the back of her hand, unable to look at the hickeys from the same choker on Missy's neck. The woman's eyes were bloodshot, and her voice was husky when she spoke.

"Here you are."

Tansi's eyes wandered up the street out of habit, surveying her surroundings with practiced necessity. She saw DJ's truck parallel parked in front of Pink Panther, exhaust still pouring out the back as it was left running. Even unattended, it was safe. No one would touch anything that belonged to DJ.

When she hesitated, Missy spoke again. "You can get out now."

Tansi stole a glance at the woman in the driver's seat, noting that she wasn't even looking at her. She seemed inconvenienced somehow, and Tansi couldn't help but wonder if she'd been disappointed in the sex. She reminded herself that Missy had been like this the first time, too. Yet sShe not only found Tansi again, but she paid her more than *anyone* else did.

"Are you trying to avoid someone?" Missy asked, eyes drifting to the truck across the street.

Tansi briskly unbuckled, grabbing the door handle. "Thanks for the ride."

She exited the car, quickly walking up the steps into the front lobby of The Palace. Once inside, she peered through the dingy glass of the front window, watching as Missy's car remained for nearly a minute before pulling away and disappearing down the street.

Tansi began the slow trek up the stairs, legs going from jelly to lead as she reached her floor and approached the door to their room. She tried to turn the knob, but the door wouldn't open.

She spoke into the crack of the door, lips brushing the union of metal and wood. "Alice?"

As she leaned in, she thought she could hear voices inside, maybe the television. She sighed, fumbling in her purse for her key. Her knuckles brushed the face of her cellphone, causing it to illuminate with a stream of missed notifications. She had lost track of time and hadn't messaged Alice, so most of the messages and calls were from her.

She found her key, squeezing the brass against her palm as she did a double take at the top two notifications.

A cold sweat covered her body, and every beat of her heart sent a shockwave of nausea and lightheadedness through her brain.

im scared

luce & ajs here. don't come

She turned to retreat, but Donnie and DJ were coming up the stairs. Tansi froze, spine becoming so rigid that she nearly bent backwards.

"Hey, Tans," DJ said with his gold smile. "Just in time for our little family meeting."

Donnie wore his own shit-eating grin, resting his cold fingers on her elbow as he turned her back towards the door. "Aren't you just lucky?"

DJ tapped his knuckles against the door, saying, "Open up, Aaron. It's me."

As though Aaron had been standing in wait, just on the other side, the door opened instantly. Aaron's blue eyes were glowing against the matching pair of shiners and they darted between Tansi's own eyes, pleading with her somehow. She didn't know what he could possibly want from her.

He was scared, and so in turn, Tansi was terrified.

Aaron moved to allow them into the apartment, the familiar sound of the door on the carpet sounding like the zipper of a body bag as the door closed behind them.

Lucy and Alice were sitting unharmed on the end of the bed. Tansi found herself releasing a relieved, but still shaky exhale. Something smelled hot; Tansi noted Alice's half-curled wig and her curling iron still plugged in on the bathroom vanity as she passed by the open door. She obviously hadn't been expecting anyone. Tansi couldn't help but wonder how the situation had unfolded.

"Have a seat, Tansi," DJ suggested, motioning towards the bed where the other two girls sat. He removed his suit jacket, handing it to Aaron, who folded it up and laid it on the back of a chair. DJ started rolling up the sleeves of his white shirt, cuffing it slowly a few inches at a time.

"I said *have a seat*," he reiterated.

Tansi obeyed this time, rushing over to seat herself between the two of them. Lucy wouldn't look at her, gaze somewhere on the floor.

DJ cleared his throat. "I've been told some really concerning things about the three of you. Things that hurt me pretty bad because I thought we were a *family*. I thought we trusted each other. Then I learn that you cunts have been trying to sneak around under my nose? The level of betrayal I feel is... well, I'm sorry, but I'm a little angry. Not just you three, but my own flesh and blood."

He turned to look at Aaron, who was rubbing his elbow nervously, refusing to make eye contact.

No one else dared to talk, so DJ continued his monologue. "So, yeah, I've been told some really troubling things. I just want to clear some shit up, while we're all here together. Wipe the slate clean, so to speak, so we can start over and get back to life as it's supposed to be, 'kay? Lucy."

Lucy didn't move when he said her name, but Tansi could feel her body tense. DJ walked over to her, grabbing her chin to force her to look up at him.

"I hear that you think that a measly couple hundred is going to make us even. Do you know how much smack I've bought you and your nasty-ass friends over the last few years? This don't even touch your debt to me, and I'm not even talking about the value of the protection and job security that I offer you... all of you. I'm afraid you might've forgotten just how much you need me, Lucy, but I'm going to remind you."

He let go of her face and reached down to grab her by the arm. As he hauled her to her feet, Tansi reached over to grab her other arm.

"No!" Tansi snarled, and the two of them jerked Lucy back and forth like a ragdoll.

"Let her go, DJ," Alice interjected desperately, wringing her hands together in her lap. "What are you doing?"

Donnie snapped his fingers impatiently, and Aaron scuttled over to the bed, grabbing Tansi's elbow to pull her away from Lucy and DJ. He wasn't really trying, more guiding her than forcing her to let go. DJ jerked Lucy away from her, swinging her into the air before he slammed her down onto the couch so forcefully that she bounced.

"Get off of me, you prick," Tansi growled, swiping at Aaron with her hands balled into fists. She felt her knuckles collide with his lip, smashing it against his teeth.

He pulled away from her suddenly, pressing his fingers to his bleeding mouth before he shoved her. The force was surprising, causing Tansi to stumble back onto the bed again before she scrambled back to her feet, rushing towards DJ as he fought to hold Lucy's arms above her head.

"Jesus Christ, AJ, *get her*," Donnie sighed, voice seething with irritation. "You stay right where you are, Alice."

Tansi felt Aaron grab her from behind again, this time with enough strength that she couldn't writhe free. Lucy's angry snarls turned into terrified wails as she saw Donnie at the counter. Tansi hadn't noticed the club owner move there, but she smelled the acrid acidity of cheap and diluted heroin being heated.

Through the hair in her face she struggled to figure out what was going on. She slung her head, gritting her teeth so firmly that they squeaked. Donnie came over to the couch after a few more moments and Lucy's screams intensified into something inhuman. DJ drowned out most of the sound by pinning his forearm against her throat, pressing his body against hers to keep her down as he fumbled for the television remote. He flipped it on and a black and white movie came on: a handsome man in a suit was chasing a woman down a rainy street; she was holding a hat to her head as the storm drenched her. Tansi wanted to tell her to keep running.

DJ mashed the volume button, and the sounds of the movie filled the room to mask the noise of the fight. Donnie held the syringe in the air as he approached the end of the couch and struggled to pull off one of Lucy's shoes and socks. He tossed the high-top ball shoe to the corner, followed by the sock with cartoon dogs on them.

Alice finally screamed. Tansi had forgotten she had existed, and she might as well have been in another universe.

"DJ! Don't do this. She's learned her lesson. You'll kill her with that. What about her baby? AJ, *what about your baby?*"

Tansi could feel Aaron's body shaking as he clutched her against him. He was squeezing her so tightly that she could feel the increased pace of his heart. No one did anything, though. Tansi even stopped struggling as she watched Donnie shove the dull needle beneath Lucy's toenail.

She was gasping now, tears pouring down her face, blue-white hair stuck to her damp cheeks. She found language again, choosing to beg "no" again and again, as though they could undo what had been done to her.

DJ lay atop her until her body relaxed, her eyes fixed somewhere on the ceiling and she let out a long exhale.

He leaned towards her ear, whispering, "We can call it even when you're dead."

He stood up beside Donnie, and they surveyed her body as it lay draped across the couch. Donnie was muttering something to DJ, laughing quietly.

Tansi couldn't look at her: the way tears still fell out of her eyes without effort, the way her toenail bulged with too much fluid, dripping blood-tinged ooze onto the floor like melting ice.

"Yeah, I mean... don't waste the easy fuck." DJ shrugged and Donnie clapped him on the back before he started unbuttoning his pants.

Tansi found another burst of energy, slinging her head back and feeling it collide with Aaron's face. He squealed, loosening his grip enough that she tore free of his arms. She lunged towards Donnie, not sure what she would do if she could get her hands on him, but willing to find out as she went. DJ caught her midway, jerking her up off the ground like he had Lucy.

Alice started her own flight, rushing towards the open bathroom door. Aaron tried to grab her, causing her to trip and fall face first into the door facing. The thud resounded in the room, even over the sound of the big band playing on the classic film. DJ dropped Tansi to the floor, shoving her down with his foot as he grabbed Aaron by the collar and dragged him to the bathroom.

"Hold her down, and don't fuck this up or I'll put you in a dumpster too."

Aaron's face was devoid of color as Tansi made eye contact with him from her place on the floor. Her right ankle and both knees ached from the impact. Despite his fear and discomfort, Aaron held Alice down on the bathroom floor. She didn't fight him at all – a stark difference between her and the other two girls. Tansi stared at her, dumfounded. She listened to her try to plead and reason, even as DJ jerked down her underwear beneath her skirt.

He reached up and grabbed the curling iron from the counter, pulling the entire length of cord down to the floor with him. He squeezed the handle, opening and closing the end like the long beak of a chomping bird.

"Open up." DJ laughed, biting his lower lip as he shoved the hot iron between her legs. The sizzle of the metal against her thighs buzzed in Tansi's skull, making her reel. Alice screamed, pulling her legs apart to avoid more contact with the hot metal, but then DJ shoved it inside her.

He laughed as he penetrated her over and over with the curling iron, blood pouring onto his hands before the accosted flesh cauterized around it. Chunks of skin clung to the end, and eventually it looked like too much tissue was hanging out of her.

Tansi struggled to her feet, so dizzy that she swayed on her feet. Instead of rushing to Alice's aid, she turned to Lucy's incapacitated form as Donnie hunkered over her with sweat beading on the back of his head. She jumped on him, wrapping her arms around his neck. She didn't know what came over her, but she bit his ear, chomping down until her teeth came together with a pop.

Someone grabbed her from behind and she was airborne. She never even felt her head hit the floor.

Eleven

It took Tansi three miserable days to recover from her injuries, and they had been the most mild. She was still plagued with a head that felt like it was full of electrified cotton and daylight-sensitive eyes.

Alice had gone to the hospital for her injuries, an *actual* hospital. She had serious burns and some kind of prolapse. They cleaned out all of the dead tissue and shoved everything back in. She had stayed at the hospital for twenty-four hours and then signed out against medical advice.

Tansi commended her for even going.

Since returning home, she was forced to wear a diaper, and Tansi kept her wounds coated in a silvery-white cream that they sent with her. Alice stayed on the phone almost constantly, trying to find Lucy.

By the time Tansi had come to after her fall, she found the apartment totally empty. No one had heard from Lucy since.

"You're sure you haven't seen her at all?" Tansi heard Alice's exasperated voice from the bed. She busied herself with her makeup in the mirror, trying to ignore the stubbornly blood-stained grout beneath her feet.

"If you see her, you call me *right away*. No, she's not in trouble. We just haven't seen her and we're worried about her. You know, her well-being."

When Alice ended the call, Tansi forced herself to wander in, sitting expectantly at the foot of the bed. They sat in silence for several minutes. Alice chewed her already ragged nails.

"Still no sign?" Tansi finally asked, looking up at her.

"No. It's just like she's disappeared into thin air." Alice breathed the words, barely audible.

"Keep trying. I'm going out."

"You're working again?"

"Alice, you know I gotta."

Alice didn't respond. DJ had made it clear that he still expected her cut, even with her serious injuries. That meant that it would come down to Tansi to make both of their wages. Luckily, the last payment from Missy already helped clear that gap.

"I'm going to look for that woman. If I can get with her again, we could be set."

"How are you going to find her?"

"Just wait, I guess. She'll show up, I think."

But Tansi didn't know that. She was desperate, almost desperate enough to get a ride to The Grand and throw herself at Missy's feet... but she knew that desire had to be part of the game, and that there was nothing desirable about desperation.

"She freaks me out a little," Tansi admitted quietly.

"You've said that, but why?"

"I don't know... just gives me the heebie-jeebies. You know... what do they call it? Where something is kind of off, looks human but your brain just knows it isn't?"

Alice paused for a few seconds. "Uncanny valley."

"Yeah. That shit."

"I'm a good judge of character," Alice said, shifting on the bed and putting a pillow beneath her knees. "I didn't get any weird vibes from her. No more weird than any other person that comes to this hellhole of their own volition."

"Yeah, maybe you're right. I'm gonna go down, see if I see that girl down there. Maybe stop in The Flamingo."

"You know I'm not one to tell you where to spend your money... but I don't know that we got a booze budget right now, sweetie."

"No..." Tansi breathed a cold laugh.

Alice tilted her chin up, jaw dropping to allow a soft "ah" to slip out.

"Ah, that guy. The speaking-talking one."

"Just need to clear my head a bit," Tansi insisted.

"Be careful out there. Keep your eyes open. I got a feeling that DJ and company aren't done punishing us yet. At this point, we may as well be disposable."

Tansi gave a grim nod before she turned, without saying goodbye, and headed out of the apartment. The neighbor from number 314 was standing in the hallway on his cellphone, cussing about what sounded like a bit of gambling gone wrong. When he noticed Tansi coming down the hall, he quickly turned and darted back into the apartment, slamming the door. He must have heard about what was going on and wanted zero trouble from DJ.

She had to wait to cross the street, and the traffic sent a shock of guilt to her gut. As she walked in front of a patient vehicle, ignoring the man calling to her out the window, her eyes flicked to the line of people in front of Pink Panther. She didn't see Donnie lurking outside, thankfully, but when the bouncer saw her crossing the street, he pointed his index finger at her and then made the motion of a gun hammer. It could have been nothing, maybe even flirty, yet his cold eyes suggested anything but.

She quickened her pace, cutting towards the Flaming-O at an angle. She didn't take a breath until she was inside the bar, shaking off the tension in her shoulders. The girl at the door tipped her head towards her.

"You okay?"

"Yeah, fine thank you," Tansi said with a smile.

The bar was buzzing as usual, and she had to shuffle around the floor to avoid bumping into anyone or stepping on any toes. The bartender saw her as she approached, and she found herself quirking a brow at them as she reached the bartop.

"Are you the only bartender that works here?"

They looked a little offended, pursing their lips together as they studied her for a moment.

"I didn't mean it like that..." Tansi said with an apologetic smile.

"Reilly's been asking about you," they said, grabbing an abandoned glass and putting it into a rack to be cleaned. "It's always 'has that girl been here?'"

"Really?" Tansi felt her cheeks flush and found herself rubbing her eye to try to mask it.

"Yeah. He's out back again."

"He spends a lot of time out back, doesn't he?"

They shrugged and motioned to the door to the side of the stage. It was gently propped open, a rim of pink light illuminating it like a neon border.

"I may just go say hi," she admitted, shrugging her shoulders like it was an afterthought.

"Please," they said with a smile.

She stopped more than once on the way to the door, the bundle of nerves in her gut growing from a gentle flutter to the wings of a too-large bird. When she pushed the door open, though, she didn't hesitate.

The light from The Strip assaulted her eyes, even in the dark alleyway. She scanned the space: dank, wet, and swampy. Next to an overfilled dumpster, Elijah crouched with a can in his hand, and a scroungy orange cat was eating from it.

Both Elijah and the cat looked up at her, almost as though they had expected someone. The cat's eyes were large and animated beneath a low brow, small features flecked with bits of patè as its rough tongue swiped over its whisker pad. It looked at her with an almost human consideration, eyes glistening in the light like they contained dozens of magenta fireflies.

"Hey," Elijah said, smiling broadly at her.

It was stupid how adorable he was with his dimpled cheeks and soft eyes. She found herself feeling childish again, and she was sure – if not for the tinted light – he could surely see the warmth in her face.

"Are you performing tonight?" she asked, motioning awkwardly over her shoulder as though he might need confirmation as to what she meant.

"I already did," he said, smile not fading. "I'd love to just sit and chat, though, if you were planning on being here for a little bit."

Tansi took a deep breath to respond, and he interrupted her softly, "No obligations or strings attached. Just eat some bar food and watch some of the other performances."

"Okay," she responded, "I think I have a little time."

She took a step away from the door to allow him to lead the way. As she moved, the cat took off down the alleyway, galloping until he was lost to the dark.

"I'm so sorry. I didn't mean to scare it away."

Elijah set the can of food under the edge of the dumpster before he stood up, shrugging. "He's a traveler— not from around here. He was never going to stay long, anyway."

He opened the door, holding it open until she awkwardly passed inside. The way it slammed behind her made her flinch, and she composed herself as he led her to a table with two chairs against the wall. It somehow seemed louder there.

"I'll get you something to drink. What do you want?" he asked, voice nearly entirely lost to the pair playing a bluesy sort of rock-rap fusion on stage.

"Just a light beer, whatever's on tap."

"What about food?"

"Oh, I'm not hungry."

He retreated towards the bar, and when his back was turned, she quickly retrieved a compact from her purse and checked her hair and make up. Only moments later, he returned, precariously carrying two glasses against his chest and a plate of nachos in one of his hands. He set the nachos down in front of her, grease pooling to one side beneath the chips as the dish tilted.

Beer sloshed onto his arm as he struggled to get the glass into his hand. He set it in front of her and put his own down before he took his seat. Just another fizzy soda.

"You don't drink?" she asked, motioning towards the glass.

"Nah," he said casually, reaching across the table with his hand. Tansi recoiled at first, but then she realized he was offering his hand to be shaken. She took it awkwardly.

"You didn't tell me your name," he said. "I'm—"

"Elijah, I remember. Tansi."

"Tansi?" he repeated, leaning towards her as he withdrew his hand.

"Yes."

"Tansi. I like that."

She didn't know how to respond, so she busied herself by sipping her beer. She hated beer, but if he was buying, she wanted to order the cheapest thing that wasn't water.

"So, Elijah," she said, watching as he took a sip of his Coke. "Are you from the area?"

"Yeah, I live in Sunning. In the inner city. I was born and raised in West Sunning – always said I'd leave but crawled just far enough away that I'm in a different zip code... and that's where I've stayed."

"You drive all the way to Jessop Terrace?"

He shrugged, picking at a swollen part of the tabletop with one of his short nails. "The Flaming-O is probably the most art-forward venue I've ever performed at. I love the people; they're family. I mean, the area isn't the greatest, but I've never been one to feel out of place in the dark."

"How do you do it? The spoken word stuff. It's kind of like poetry or like you're saying song lyrics or something."

"There is nothing to it. All you do is stand there and bleed." He took another sip and winked at her. "Hemingway. Sort of."

"Is this what you do professionally? Like for work?"

He laughed. "I wish. I'm also an artist... which doesn't pay the bills, either. Actually, it really costs me more money than I ever get from it... so I'm a janitor at Sunning General. Isn't glamorous, but I just work a couple of days a week, and I can kind of keep to myself. Listen to music, daydream."

"That sounds nice, actually."

"What about you?"

"What?" Tansi blinked.

"Are you from here? Where do you work?"

She could easily answer the first one. She would tell him about every mile she had ever traveled if it meant she could avoid talking to him about the second question. She thought about lying, but that just added a level of complication, something you had to keep adding layers to so that you couldn't see the ugly truth beneath. She could tell him she was an escort or a cam girl; usually those were two more readily accepted (and sometimes even admired) facets of the larger industry in which she worked. Often, the girls who had those jobs were independent, powerful, in control... free. What Tansi did was something else entirely.

"I'm not from here," she finally said with a small smile. "Small-town girl. I do live here now, though. *Here*. On The Strip. Actually, I share an apartment with a friend at The Palace."

She watched his expression with sick intensity. He didn't seem to react in a negative way – or at all – to her admission that she lived here in what he described as "the dark."

"Small-town girl, huh? Big difference coming to Sunning... even bigger ending up here. How long have you been here?"

"Too long," she breathed a laugh.

"Do you work nearby?"

Tansi's hands quivered beneath the table. She looked over her shoulder at the door as she responded, "Um. Yeah, pretty close by. Hey, I've had a great time chatting with you, but I just realized I've got to go do something."

"Oh, okay," he said, standing as she did.

She looked down at their half-finished drinks and the untouched plate of nachos, and she hated herself. She blamed herself. She resented every decision she had made that brought her to this moment. If only she'd met him in a different life, maybe he could have liked her; maybe he could have *loved* her, even.

He followed her out onto the street. She stood awkwardly across from him, clutching the strap of her purse with one hand.

"So, if this wasn't too miserable for you, I'd love to take you out for a drink. Somewhere else, though," he finally said, face illuminated by the neon flamingo above them. The light didn't find any shadows to draw from his face, even adding a glossy brightness to his eyes.

"I thought you didn't drink?"

She noticed a car pull along the sidewalk, and she knew with just a glance that it was Keistyn from fEmpower. She would sit there and wait patiently, without an ounce of hurry. Another layer of stress coated Tansi's gut.

Elijah's eyes shifted to the car as hers did but quickly focused back on her face as he smiled again. "Only the good stuff. I can pick you up in front of The Palace. Friday, seven o'clock?"

That would be another night of missed money. She should decline, but everything in her wanted to say yes.

Then he surprised her.

"It looks like you've got to get back to work, and I get it," he said, backing away slowly. "But just say yes?"

"O-okay." She stammered the word, but she couldn't stop the smile that matched his.

"Okay. Friday, seven. Oh... and wear pants and real shoes."
"Why?" she asked, puzzled.

"Friday at seven," he repeated, walking down the street with his hands in his pockets until he began disappearing into the dark.

Tansi turned to face the next hurdle, but she felt there wasn't much that could sour this mood.

Keistyn rolled the window down as Tansi approached, but she continued watching Elijah's retreating form in her side mirror. "Did I make you lose one?"

"Nah, he's not like that. He's different."

Keistyn tipped her chin up in a reverse nod before she fixed her eyes on Tansi's. "Have you been in contact with Miss Lucy?"

Tansi was never as good at masking her emotions as she wanted to be. She swallowed and reached up to rub her nose, trying to look as casual as possible.

"Last I heard, she was with you." Tansi forced herself to look at Keistyn as she spoke.

"We've got her all set up. Place to stay, clean clothes. She's got an interview at a temp agency next week."

"Good for her. I'm glad she's got something going for her."

"She had a prenatal appointment a few days ago. She missed the appointment. No one has seen or heard from her since. I thought maybe you might have seen her if she came back down here."

Tansi shifted, crossing her arms over her gut. "She'd have to be stupid to come back here."

"She's just a kid. You're just a kid."

Tansi rolled her eyes. "I'm not as young as you think I am."

"Honey, I've got addictions older than you," Keistyn snapped, leaning towards the window until the light shone off of the bronze highlighter on her cheeks and the gold lipstick on her mouth.

"I haven't seen Lucy," Tansi repeated.

They stared at each other for a few moments, and finally Keistyn resorted to sighing and putting her car in gear.

"You still got my number, don't you?"

"I do," Tansi said. "Stuck to the fridge."

A commotion just down the street drew the attention of both women. Coming out of Pink Panther was Donnie. He was smoking a cigarette like he was pissed at it, dragging so hard that his cheeks sank in. There was a blond-tinged bandage on his ear, the one she'd nearly bitten off. His eyes went straight for her, and he reached up to pinch the cigarette delicately between his middle and index fingers before he raised the other hand and made a "come here" motion at her.

Tansi would have dived into Keistyn's car if the woman hadn't noticed Donnie's appearance as well.

"Looks like you gotta go," Keistyn said. "If you see her, give me a call. I still want to help her. She *wanted* us to help her. It's hard to see them backslide like this. If you care about that girl, you tell me when you know something."

"Alright," Tansi said with a nod.

Keistyn's car was in motion, and Tansi watched it pull away, feeling a cool chill crawl across her scalp. She couldn't run. There was nowhere in Jessop Terrace that Donnie couldn't find her if he wanted to.

She walked towards him at the slowest pace she thought she could get away with. His face was obscured by smoke until the moment she was within reach of him. The Panther's lights were just a little harsher than those of the Flaming-O, leaving a darker, nearly red dye on everything within its reach.

"Yeah, Donnie?"

"Need to get your payment for the week," Donnie said, putting the cigarette between his teeth again.

"You don't ever collect for DJ." Tansi said, brow furrowing. "I don't have all of it with me right now, but—"

He was faster than he looked. His hand was around her throat in an instant: a fleshy, adorned viper thet cupped her beneath her jaw. His fingers squeezed against the hinged bone, making a grinding sound in her ears.

"Give me what you've got on you, and I'll get the rest later."

Tansi tried to look down, but he held her there, so she fumbled for her purse without looking. By feel, she found the small wallet inside and thumbed out every bill she could. She held it up, and Donnie took it with his free hand, shoving it into the deep pocket of his slacks.

Then he took the short cigarette out of his mouth and extinguished it on her neck. The flame bit into the flesh, leaving a crisp and burning hickey. She choked back a squeal of pain, watching the fury in Donnie's eyes when she didn't scream like he wanted her to. She couldn't stop the rogue tears, one from each eye, that dripped down her cheeks. He let her go, and she stumbled away from him, into the road. She didn't even look for traffic.

"Hey, Donnie," she snarled. "Hope the rest of your fucking ear rots off."

He didn't come after her, but she could tell he wanted to. She turned her back on him, trying to act like she wasn't afraid he might follow her... but she listened for the sounds of his designer shoes behind her until she was safe behind the locked door of her apartment.

Twelve

"How does it look?" Alice asked, looking at Tansi between her thighs like she was delivering a baby.

Tansi didn't really know what to tell her. It looked *like shit*. Considering she'd been violated with a hot curling iron, she supposed it looked okay. Where the tissue wasn't red and irritated, it was yellow-brown with papules that oozed clear and clearish fluid. Alice said she'd read online as long as the fluid was clear and didn't have an odor, it was a normal part of healing.

But having a cunt that looked like fire-roasted cauliflower was *not* normal.

Tansi bit her lip.

"That bad?"

"No... I think it looks better. It's just hard to say, I don't know what it's supposed to look like at this point. Does it hurt?"

Alice shrugged, "Honestly, I don't feel much of anything right now."

Maybe she wouldn't ever feel anything again.

"What about this little thing sticking out here? Is that supposed to be there?"

There was the tiniest piece of pink that pushed out of the bottom of her slit like a partially rolled tongue. It looked like the healthiest tissue in the entire area.

"I think that's just part of the prolapse left over. A little part that keeps coming out. I don't know."

"I think you should go let a doctor check it again, Alice. Just to be safe."

Alice sat up slowly, folding her legs together with great caution. Her short, dark hair was messy and oily. She'd really let the rest of her self-care fall by the wayside since the incident.

"That lady from fEmpower stopped me last night. Looking for Lucy." Tansi said, voice quiet.

"What did you tell her?"

"That I haven't seen her."

"So she hasn't either?"

Tansi shook her head.

They sat in silence for several moments, and just as Alice opened her mouth to say something, there was a knock at the door. Neither of them moved to open it, both staring straight ahead at the entry and waiting to make sure they'd really heard it.

Another knock.

Tansi stood and slowly made her way over to the door, peering out the peephole to see a bubble-version of DJ's bottom bitch: Trixie.

"It's Trixie," Tansi whispered to Alice.

"What's she want?"

"I don't know..."

She didn't unlock the chain but instead cracked the door open as far as it would go, looking Trixie up and down with an expression of unmasked disgust. "Yeah?"

"Here to collect for DJ. He says you got your cut and Alice's too," she said, chewing a wad of gum obnoxiously as she spoke. Tansi could tell it was rubbery and overused. There was no pleasant smell anymore, and Trixie's jaw popped with every motion.

"Donnie took it yesterday."

"Donnie don't collect for DJ," Trixie said, not missing a beat.

Tansi set her jaw. "Well, he did yesterday."

"So you don't have anything. That's the message you want me to pass on for you?"

"Trixie, ask Donnie. He'll tell you. I gave him everything I had last night."

"How about you talk to him yourself? DJ's at The Panther too. Let's take a walk."

Tansi hesitated, but Trixie's blue eyes never left hers. It was almost as though Trixie knew exactly how this conversation was going to go, like Tansi was being set up. She didn't like that feeling: the cold, weighty stone of fear settling in her gut.

"Let me grab my purse; I'll meet you downstairs."

"Don't fuck around. I've got shit to do," Trixie snapped, turning on her heels before Tansi had the opportunity to shut the door in her face.

"What's that about?" Alice asked, face taking on a nervous pallor.

"Last night, Donnie stopped me outside The Flamingo and told me he was collecting for DJ. Took everything I had."
She reached up and scratched the fresh scab on her neck.

"You don't got to go down there. I can call DJ... see what's going on. I don't like the way this feels."
"How's it feel?"

"Like they're playing with you."

"I'll be alright." Tansi offered her the empty assurance. As she headed downstairs to meet Trixie, she considered whether they *were* playing with her, which meant only two things could be possible: either they were trying to scare her into never crossing DJ again, or they had already marked her off as dead-in-the-water, and would make an example of her to other girls.

Crossing the street with Trixie felt more like passing over the river Styx into the Underworld than anything else. She found herself shivering with anxiety as they approached the line outside of Pink Panther. The bouncer nodded at Trixie as she tossed her hand in the air, grabbing Tansi by the wrist as though their connection would be the only way she could slip inside the door.

The interior of the club was loud and crowded. The erratic flashing of lights, coupled with the soulless thud of some instrumental dubstep, was disorienting. Women with fake smiles took spiked drinks from men who looked like they had money. They'd wake up in the morning and find that not only was he broke, but now she was too.

Trixie moved through the crowd with her long fingers still clamped around Tansi's wrist. The sharp nails pressed gently against her flesh like a warning. No one moved aside for the two girls, but they slipped through like water and skirted along the dance floor.

Tansi tried not to make eye contact with the glassy stare of the drunk men who gently rocked at the edge of the floor with drinks in their hands. She recognized so many of them.

Up a small flight of stairs, she could already see DJ sitting on a round couch in the corner, surrounded by a group of men and women who were laughing with forced amusement at whatever he was saying. Donnie was on the end with a woman under each arm as he belly-laughed with a bray like a horse.

"Trixie," DJ said with a broad smile, "and is that Tansi? Have a seat, girls. Let me introduce you to some of my friends."

Tansi grabbed her own arm as her eyes panned the faces of the people who sat around them. DJ rattled off their names and what made them important: all of the women were with someone, never given any identifier beyond a first name and which male counterpart claimed them at the moment. It soured Tansi's tongue.

"Now that introductions are out of the way, what can I do for you, Trix?" he asked.

"Just brought her by to clear something up," she said, and Tansi envied the cool and confident way she addressed DJ. She'd give Trixie that: the girl was fearless, which was probably how she'd gotten into this position. The bottom bitch was the worst of the worst, though, a woman who worked against her fellow woman.

"Something we need to talk about in private, or can it be discussed in front of friends?" DJ asked, eyes wandering over to Tansi. She pinched her tongue between her teeth to maintain her composure. Saliva pooled underneath in anticipation of pain.

"Probably a private conversation. Donnie too."

Trixie didn't put any effort into projecting volume, but her voice carried easily, even in the chaos of the club. Tansi noted Donnie and DJ exchanging glances, and they excused themselves from their company.

The girls followed them up another flight of stairs, this one stopping so close to the ceiling that Tansi thought she might be able to jump up and touch it if she tried hard enough. They were able to survey the dance floor and bar from up here, watching as the bodies below moved like feral animals gathered around a valuable resource. The height was nauseating, and Tansi found herself wavering, so she clung close to the wall, brushing shoulders with Trixie as they were led into one of the club boxes.

Pink Panther had an exclusive club where members paid a monthly fee to get into private parties, most featuring plenty of illegal activity.

Gambling, dog fighting, prostitution, even rumors of much more violent acts... it was all just another way to cash in on society's need to control and destroy; if there was anything that Donnie was good at, it was squeezing every dirty dollar out of anyone who crossed paths with him.

The interior of the club box was dark and quiet. The only light was a dull pink strip of neon that bordered the ceiling, casting dark shadows around every angle and curve of their faces. DJ took a seat on the plush couch, followed by Donnie and Trixie. Tansi stood awkwardly, without a spot.

"Come here and have a seat," DJ said, patting his lap.

"I'm really okay to stand," Tansi insisted. "I'm hoping this can be cleared up pretty fast."

"Oh, Tansi. Come on now," DJ said, frowning deeply and shaking his head. "There's no hard feelings about the other night, right? I mean... you know we gotta do what we gotta do in this business, am I right? If there's no order... there's chaos. If there's chaos, how will I take care of you?"

Tansi shifted on her feet, eyes hot with the threat of tears. She wouldn't cry in front of him. She refused.

"There's no hard feelings here," she said, voice cracking.

"That's my good girl – now, come over here."

He patted his lap again, extending his arm. Tansi reluctantly approached, sitting carefully on his thigh. There wasn't enough meat on him to be comfortable, and she felt herself sliding off either side until he jerked her towards him, forcing her to lean into his torso as he wrapped his arm around her waist to hold her tight.

"So, what's this problem we need to talk about, Trixie?"

"Tansi don't have your money."

DJ laughed a little, brow furrowing as he looked up at Tansi, but she observed that he didn't look surprised. "What? I know better than that. This has to be some kind of misunderstanding, right? Tansi knows how important it is for her *and* Alice to get their money in on time. Right, Tansi?"

"I gave my money to Donnie last night," Tansi said, eyes boring a hole into the side of Donnie's head as he sipped his gin from a faceted glass.

Donnie's brows rose. He set the glass on the table in front of him and held his gaudy fingers in the air, palms out.

"I don't know what you're talking about, Tans. I haven't seen you since the night at the apartment." Donnie smiled a toothy grin at her, reaching up to scratch his bandaged ear with his thumb.

"I *told* you Donnie don't collect for DJ," Trixie reiterated.

"What are you, a broken fucking record?" Tansi snapped.

She felt DJ squeeze the flesh of her side gently and resisted the urge to say more.

"She's right, though," DJ said, turning from Tansi to Donnie. "Donnie, be straight with me: did you pick up Tansi's money?"

"Nah, DJ. That's your business, not mine."

DJ knew.

Tansi could tell, without a doubt, that DJ knew Donnie had taken her money. Alice was right: they were playing with her.

She put on a smile, rolling her eyes and shrugging her shoulders once. "You know, I think I made a mistake. I can get you the money next week, how about that? I must have misplaced it... but I'm sure it'll turn up."

"You know I'm patient and generous." DJ sighed. "We'll just add a little interest for the delay, how about that?"

"Alright, DJ. That seems fair. How much?"

DJ regarded her for a few moments, gritting his teeth. He reached up and rubbed his thumb along her lips, pressing so hard that she felt the need to pull away, but she knew better. The sensation of his skin on hers made her gut crawl, bile rolling up her throat.

"I wouldn't take more money from you, Tansi. When you swing by and drop off what you owe me, we'll work out the interest."

"I just need to know how much I need to bring," Tansi said, clearing her throat.

"What's with the worry?" He laughed. "I wouldn't ask you to do anything you haven't done hundreds of times before."

"Okay."

She didn't know she said the word, mind fixating on the silence of the room. The boxes seemed to shut out everything else, leaving a quiet place for people to get special treatment.

"Now, see? We've got that all worked out. No hurt feelings, everyone is happy. So get out there and do what you do best."

DJ forced her to rise her feet, smacking her on the ass as she stumbled around the table and towards the door. When she opened it, she was bombarded with the strobe lights and loud music. She had to get out of here before she threw up.

She held tight to the railing as she made her way down the first flight of stairs. She scanned the crowd for the most direct path out, and that was when she saw someone standing in the shadows of the back corner, barely visible – if not for the gentle illumination of the red exit sign.

It was Missy. She was dressed in another tight black dress, this one with straps but a deep plunge between her breasts. Her eyes and painted lips were part of the darkness, almost giving her the appearance of wearing a mask.

What was she doing here?

Tansi's heart skipped a beat when she realized that Missy was watching her. From all the way across the room, she had *been* watching her. Tansi hurried down the stairs, shoving her way through the bodies on the dance floor. Drunk people pulsed and writhed like maggots, movements out of sync with the synth beat of the music.

When she breached the other side of the crowd, Missy was gone. There was nothing but a dark, empty corner where she had once stood. Tansi wondered if she'd imagined her being there.

She pushed through the exit, emerging into the unlit alleyway behind Pink Panther. It was the same alleyway where she had found Elijah feeding the stray cat, just several yards down. In the colossal shadow of the multilevel club, the alley was even darker than the area directly behind the Flaming-O.

"With friends like those…"

Tansi spun around when she heard Missy's voice, finding her standing with her back against the wall. She looked out of place in the alleyway: clean and picturesque in the grime of the street.

"…who needs enemies?" she finished, tilting her chin upwards ever so slightly. She looked as though she might smile, but she didn't. Her full lips parted only enough for Tansi to glimpse pink flesh behind the ebony lipstick.

"They're not friends," Tansi said, pulling a compact out of her purse to check her face. Her own pink lipstick was smeared around her mouth, leaving a Cheshire Cat smudge up her cheek. She licked her thumb and began diligently wiping it away.

"Do they hurt you?" she asked.

Tansi closed the compact with a loud click, dropping it back into her purse as she looked up at her.

"Who doesn't?"

"Would you want them to die?"

The way she asked it was so casual, so emotionless. Her eyes studied Tansi in the dark.

"Hey, you need anything tonight?" Tansi asked, walking towards Missy with what she hoped was a seductive sway. "I don't have anything going on, could do whatever you want. All night."

Missy turned her body towards Tansi, but she had never looked more disinterested. It was impossible to read her emotions, because there *weren't fucking any.*

"Answer my question."

"Why? You gonna kill them for me?"

"Do you want me to?"

Tansi scoffed. "Listen, this weird-ass fantasy of yours is kind of creepy."

"Humor me."

"Well, let's talk some fucking details, then. What do you do? Cut their dicks off?"

Tansi noted a faint hint of irritation in Missy's eyes. The briefest flash of annoyance.

"That's so childish. No, of course not."

"Well, if you *really* kill people and you're asking for my wishlist like some homicidal fucking Missus Claus, I want you to cut DJ's dick off when you do him for me. Oh, and I also want his ball sack so I can keep change in it." She laughed.

Missy, however, looked at her with a somber expression. "If that's what you want."

"I want that more than anything in the world."

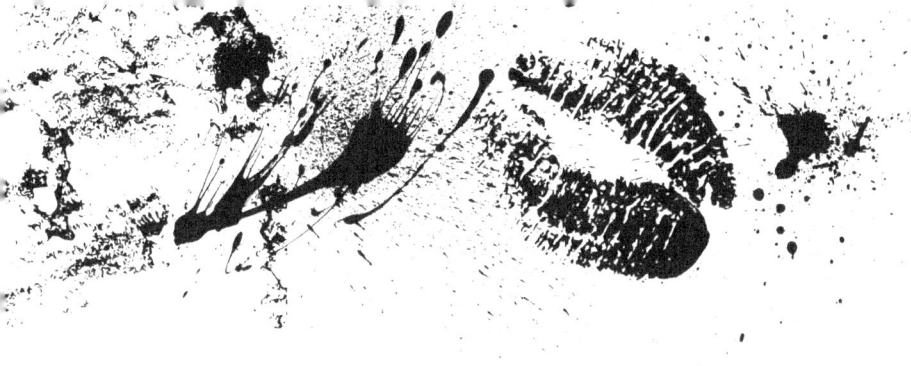

MEN WERE EASY.

In all aspects, they were simple and uncomplicated, devoid of complexity. That was one of the reasons she was so good at what she did.

Within just a few minutes, she could usually tell if the man was drawn to vulnerability or confidence. She could flip the switch before they ever realized it was a ruse. She had watched DJ leave his apartment and knew – before he even noticed her presence – he wanted her vulnerable. Missy had to do a little bit of research, figuring out which of the two men from the club was DJ. She quickly discovered that the other man was named Donnie, and he owned the club.

Missy had been pleasantly surprised when Tansi hadn't reacted to her presence at the club with suspicion. For Missy, that meant she knew she was being stalked, and she was okay with it. That meant that she was likely willing to be complicit.

Missy followed DJ to a disgusting bar just a block from his apartment building. She hadn't expected him to wander away from Jessop Terrace, where all of the activity was, but she was pleased with less traffic. People moved away from him on the street, giving him a wide berth, as though he had some kind of reputation.

At first, she thought she might have missed her opportunity. When she slipped inside the smoky interior, choked by a haze of tobacco and weed, she saw DJ was already at the bar and sidling up to a girl who was hovering over a still-full beer. The girl wasn't interested, and when she made eye contact with the bartender, they suggested she come to the other end of the bar, away from DJ. He didn't have the same power here, and judging by the way his knuckles turned white with pressure as the girl moved away, he didn't like it.

Temper, temper.

This was her chance. She walked over, sitting next to him as she pretended to wait for the bartender's return. She made sure that when she sat down, her dress rode up just the slightest amount, exposing what seemed like a bit more thigh than was intended. Her brows softened, lips pulling taut at the corners. Even the way she touched her face and fiddled with her hair was part of her carefully crafted persona.

She felt his eyes on her almost immediately, and if she hadn't felt them, she would've smelled the booze on his breath. Obviously drunk before he'd ever stepped foot inside this establishment, he wasn't here for the alcohol; he was here for the prey.

And here she was.

She tilted her chin towards him just a little, hair falling across her cheek as she gave an embarrassed cringe, "Hi. Just... trying to get a drink. I'm so sorry, was someone sitting here?"

DJ snapped his fingers at the bartender, who turned and looked at him with obvious disgust.

"Hey," DJ slurred. Oh, he was *so* drunk already. "This lady wants something to drink. Do your fucking job, why don't you?"

The bartender sauntered over, leaning onto the counter in front of her expectantly.

"I... oh, I don't know what I want." Her eyes darted to DJ. "I'm such a lightweight. What's something that doesn't taste super alcohol-y?"

"Go big or go home, little lady," DJ laughed, drenching her in a smog of booze breath. "Get her a tequila soda, splash of cranberry."

The bartender looked at her for confirmation, and she smiled broadly, nodding.

"Sure, I'll try that."

"Put it on my tab," DJ said, winking at her.

"Oh, you don't have to do that!" Missy exclaimed, hand hovering over her dark lips in surprise.

"I insist," he responded.

She sipped the drink and hummed a satisfied "mmmm" in her throat, followed by a fake cough.

"A little strong."

"What's a girl like you doing on this end of town?" DJ asked, tossing back another glass of beer like it was water.

"Oh, it's embarrassing…" Missy said, voice quiet. She looked at the bar between them, tucking her hair behind her ear.

"I won't laugh."

"My boyfriend broke up with me today. We have been dating for six months, and he left me for someone with…" –she looked around and then leaned in to whisper– "…more experience."

"That fucker."

"So I was upset and took a cab, ended up here on accident… but I needed to have a good time tonight. I'm glad I ended up here. You seem like such a good guy."

She reached across the bar and touched her fingers to his thigh. He looked at the contact, and she knew from that stupid glimmer in his eyes that she had him hooked.

Checkmate, you stupid piece of shit.

"You want to get out of here?" he asked.

Missy pulled her purse into her lap. "Really? Like... me and you?"

"Yeah," DJ said, shrugging like he was doing her a favor.

"Oh... I don't know," Missy drawled on, unzipping the purse and pretending to dig through it.

"I told you, I got the drink," he reiterated, and she thought she detected a little more temper on his tongue.

She waited until the bartender was on the other end of the bar, helping the girl from earlier, and then she quickly said, "Well, okay. Let's go have some fun. I deserve to have fun, right?"

"You bet your ass you do," DJ said, standing up to lean across the bar and yell obnoxiously at the back of the bartender's head.

Missy quickly pulled two stray pills out of her purse, dumping them into what remained of her vodka soda. She swirled the drink in her hand and waited for DJ and the bartender to stop bickering.

"Hey," Missy said, grabbing DJ's arm gently.

He turned to look at her. She slid her glass across the bartop. "I'm really dizzy, I don't even know if I can walk out of here. Will you finish this off, pretty please?"

He seemed annoyed, but he grabbed the glass and turned it up, draining every drop of liquid into his mouth. He slammed the glass down so hard that she thought it might have cracked.

The bartender purposefully took a solid fifteen minutes seeing to the other patrons. Missy was patient, and the longer the drink sat in DJ's gut the better. He was sweating, veins bulging in both his head and neck from the fury at being made to wait.

When the bartender wandered over, he pushed the buttons on the register with such a deliberate lack of speed that Missy found herself amused.

"Hurry *the fuck* up," DJ barked, slurring his words.

"Forty-nine bucks."

"How the fuck is it forty-nine dollars?"

"Do you really want me to tell you how many beers you've had? Pay up and take a hike."

DJ slung a fifty dollar bill across the bar, forcing the bartender to pick it up from the floor.

"Keep the fucking change, you useless prick," DJ snarked.

When DJ stood up, his knees buckled beneath him, and he fell to the floor. People turned to look, but no one moved to help him. He struggled onto his hands and knees, trying to get to his feet with shaky effort.

Missy pouted and looked at the bartender, "Could someone help him outside? My car is parked right around the corner."

"Anything to get that prick out of here," the bartender muttered, politely informing a few of the customers that he would be right back.

He rounded the bar and roughly hoisted DJ to his feet. He acted like he was cumbersome, despite the fact that he was probably a foot-and-a-half taller and bore fifty more pounds of muscle.

"Where are we going?" DJ slurred, saliva dripping from his mouth.

"Just to my car. It's okay, I'll get you taken care of," Missy cooed.

"He's sloshed," the bartender grunted as Missy unlocked the car, rushing ahead to open the passenger door. He poured DJ into the seat, even leaning down to throw his legs and feet into the floorboard before slamming the door shut.

"Good luck," he huffed, disappearing down the street.

Missy leaned against the vehicle until the bartender was out of sight, then she walked around to the other side of the car. She checked the street, drenched in yellow light for a moment. The golden sheen melted off of her skin as she descended into the darkness of the car. DJ's smell was nauseating. Men had this odor, even when they were clean and tried to hide it. DJ was not one of those men who tried to hide it. Coupled with the overwhelming aroma of cheap beer and bile. Missy forced herself to crack the windows.

DJ grumbled from the seat, "I thought you took a cab?"

"I didn't say that," she assured him as she put the car in reverse and drove down the street. The farther she drove, the darker the city became. These areas were just on the fringe of civilization: reclaimed by an urban ferality. She drove behind an old factory building that the locals said had been renovated into a music venue before their liquor license was revoked. Now it was completely empty, just another skeletal remnant in the forgotten part of Sunning.

An old parking garage – one that echoed every sound and vibrated as her car ascended –stood out back: a reminder that once this place had plenty of visitors.

She put the car in park on the top floor, surveying what little bit of the old parts of the city were visible. It could've been a convincing backdrop to a post-apocalyptic film. She took a deep breath, turning to look at DJ. He had regained some of his composure, sitting upright and blinking wildly.

"Where are we?"

Missy smiled, sheepish.

"You said you wanted to have fun with me, didn't you?"

"Yeah, but..." He blinked again. "Fuck, there's something wrong with my eyes."

"Had a little too much to drink, didn't you?"

"I think I need a few minutes before... You know, I think I need to go to a bathroom."

"Don't worry about *performing*. I have some of these."

She reached into her purse and withdrew a metal tin. It had once housed mints, and when she opened the top the smell of mint mingled with the stench of the man in the passenger seat. Her manicured nails tapped against the metal as she reached inside and withdrew a small berry. It was as black as her nail polish and with a surface just as shiny.

"What are those?" He asked, still blinking at her as though he couldn't tell exactly where she was.

"They're an aphrodisiac."

"An afro what?"

"No, silly." She giggled, leaning across the center console. Her lips hovered near his. She reached up with her free hand to place her thumb on his chin. His mouth opened, and she popped a berry inside.

He chewed slowly, and then she fed him another and another.

"Making my mouth dry," he muttered.

"Yeah, but making your cock hard, isn't it?" she asked, grasping a handful of his semi-erect dick through his pants. He moaned but tried to jerk away from her, and she saw a little bit of fear in his eyes for the first time.

She hadn't expected DJ to be so easy. As afraid as everyone seemed to be of him, he hadn't been difficult to trap.

He leaned in towards her, trying to kiss her on the mouth, but she dodged his advances and he fell face first into her shoulder. She shoved him back into his seat.

"I thought you'd be more fun." She sighed. "The way everyone talks about you, looks at you— I thought I was after some big game this time, but here you are... just a sad little boy."

"Who the fuck are you, bitch?" he snapped, sitting up straighter. He swung a fist at her, *actually tried to punch her*, but he was moving in slow motion. She dodged it as easily as she had his kiss, grabbing his balled fingers in her own and offering it a firm squeeze.

"You're not the first one, and you won't be the last one. I've got my eyes on that disgusting pig that owns the club too."

"I'm not what? You gonna rob me?"

"Yes," she admitted, "but not before I kill you."

DJ pulled the door handle, stumbling out and vomiting on the ground. She heard his wrists crack from the awkward fall, but he continued to try to get to his feet.

"Crazy fucking cunt. You think you can rob *me?*" he barked as Missy rounded the backside of the vehicle. He was on his feet, the top half of his body still hanging over like it had deflated. His voice was husky and raw. "Do you know who I am?"

She opened the back door and retrieved a wooden baseball bat from the floorboard. She pushed her hair back out of her face and hoisted the fabric of her dress farther up on her tits to avoid one falling out when she started swinging.

"I know exactly who you are. You're the same as all the rest of them. Just another face slapped on a cycle of abuse and—" She paused. "I'm just so disappointed with every single one of you. Each one is stupider and more cocky than the last. Such a high pedestal, such a long, long fall."

DJ growled and lunged at her. Although he was faster than she anticipated, he was still too high to maintain any coordination to fight her. He grabbed the dress, but she shoved him away, swinging the bat into the side of his head.

The sound was so satisfying, echoing in the air around them, followed by the howls of fury and pain.

"What the fuck... what did you do to me?"

"Pregamed you with a couple roofies. Ironically, probably from the same dealer you get your little forget-me-nots from... Then, the berries?" She squatted down. "Belladonna. If I don't kill you, she is already working on it."

As if on cue, DJ began screaming, swiping at his arms and clawing at the flesh. The side of his head swelled, obscuring his eye, but he still kicked and squirmed on the ground as though he were being eaten alive by insects.

"What do you see? What are they?"

"Get them off of me! Fuck! Someone help me! Help!"

Missy laughed and stood, holding her arms up and screaming into the night air as she spun around.

"You know better than anyone that no one can hear us out here. Isn't this place perfect? I don't have to worry about keeping anyone quiet. I can take my time. Scream as loud as you want; I love it. This is my wilderness and, baby, I'm the big bad wolf in this story. I am going to swallow—" She jabbed him with the end of the bat in his chest, causing him to skitter away from her towards the edge of the building. "You—" Another jab and his back was to the short wall. "Up." She placed the bat underneath his chin as he stared at her through blown out pupils. Blood poured down the purple half of his face, and he seemed to have forgotten the invisible creatures on his body as he stared down the length of the bat at her.

She put both hands on the handle, squeezing it as she swung it over her shoulder and back down into DJ's face. Golden teeth flew out of his mouth onto the pavement, glistening in the moonlight like shattered glass. The next blow came to the top of his head, caving in his skull and causing him to fall face first at her feet. His body convulsed and twitched on the ground, and he let out a crackling and shaky moan.

"Music to my ears." She sighed, dropping the bat to the ground with a clatter.

She reached down and hoisted him onto the edge of the parking garage wall, allowing his upper half to hover in the air.

"Did you know that the human body only contains a little more than a gallon of blood? Imagine dropping a jug of milk… that's all that you're going to leave behind. Not even that much, actually. I'll meet you down there, I've got a special request to fulfill. Hope you don't need your dick in hell."

She let him go, watching as his body seemed to teleport from her hands to the ground in an instant.

Thirteen

Things had been quiet, and despite the reprieve from harassment, Tansi didn't like it. It was Friday night, and she was more nervous than she had ever been: standing outside The Palace in a pair of blue jeans, faded sneakers, and a band t-shirt that she forgot she had. She was more nervous than she thought she'd ever been as she waited for Elijah to pick her up – both nervous that he'd not show up and that DJ or Donnie would see her standing on the street and approach her.

Donnie and DJ hadn't shown their faces again since that night at The Panther. Tansi had seen Trixie roam the street more than once, but she didn't yet approach her or confront her for money.

Three days. Tansi had three days to come up with the remaining cash. She'd been busting her ass, taking clients she didn't want and doing things she regretted, but she was desperate. Missy hadn't given her any money in the alleyway, and she hadn't seen her since. More than the money, though, she dreaded what DJ might want her to do for the "interest."

Tansi checked her phone. It was five after. Her gut sank, and she looked up and down both sides of the street. She didn't know what Elijah drove or if he might be coming to get her in a cab. Her eyes scanned the tinted windows of every vehicle that passed, but none of them were him. She glanced up at the window of her apartment, and she saw Alice perched there, watching her.

"I'm so stupid," Tansi whispered to herself, sitting down on the stairs of The Palace. "So stupid."

She dropped her purse to the ground beside her and sank her cheeks into her palms as she rested her elbows on her knees. A motorcycle drove down the street, weaving among parked and moving cars. The sound of the engine reverberated between the buildings of The Strip. It pulled up in front of The Palace. The driver dismounted and removed his helmet.

"Sorry I'm late."

Tansi's head snapped up, and she saw Elijah standing there. He tucked the helmet against his side, running a gloved hand through his hair, which was somehow even messier than it was during his performances. "Oh, that's—" Her words halted. She smiled, standing up. "You didn't tell me we'd be riding a bike."

"Yeah, I thought it was best to just tell you to dress for the ride and surprise you, so you'd still show up." He smiled back at her.

"That's not a creeper move at all. What else are you hiding from me?"

He laughed, reaching into one of the hard-shell saddlebags on the back of the bike and producing another helmet. He set his own helmet on the sidewalk while helping her slip the extra onto her head. She felt a brief moment of claustrophobia as she entered the full-face helmet, and then he reached under her chin to snap the clasp.

"I feel like an astronaut," she said.

He knocked on the top of the helmet with his fist. "A cute astronaut."

"But you can't see my face."

He took off his leather jacket and offered it to her, but she hesitated.

"Put it on; it gets chilly. Cool t-shirt... you like The Destroying Angels?"

She tried to look down at her own shirt, like she'd forgotten what she was wearing. The unexpected weight of the helmet made her tip forward until she regained her balance. Elijah already had his helmet back on.

"I can put your purse in the saddlebags. Not much room on bikes like this, but it'll fit."

She let him have the purse and put on the jacket, just a hair too large but still warm from his body. It smelled faintly of cardamom and lemon: a mixture of his cologne and maybe a cleaning product that clung to his skin after work. She wanted to dip her nose into the collar and inhale, but that was impossible with the helmet.

Elijah mounted the bike and tapped the seat behind him as he knocked the stand up and titled the bike upright.

"Is there really enough room for me back there?"

He nodded his head, and she walked over, struggling to get on behind him. She hoped he couldn't feel her heart pounding in her chest as she was forced to lean into him. He took her hands and put them around his waist, then patted her wrists before he set the motorcycle into motion with no warning.

Tansi kept her head down at first, watching the pavement rush underneath them. The neon lights made the puddles in the pavement look like glimpses into a pink hell beneath a shattered highway, but the farther from The Strip they drove, the better she felt. Elijah had been right; the air was cold, chilling her fingers to the point that she found herself slipping them under the hem of his shirt to press them against the warm flesh of his stomach. She felt his spine stiffen at the surprise of the cold, but he relaxed and reached down to lay his hand over hers for a brief moment.

She really wished he hadn't done that – having one hand off the steering was terrifying for her. She blew a long breath out of her lips, trying to relax as they coasted along the highway, covered in a blue film from the quiet night of Sunning, broken up by the bright white of street lamps. She rested her chin on his shoulder from her elevated position, helmets clacking together briefly.

They were coasting downtown: bustling with life, but not the same kind that she was used to on Jessop Terrace. These people seemed to be full of warmth and vitality; the city seemed washed out and saturated all at the same time. Her eyes felt like they'd been burned with the tones of The Strip, like looking into the sun for too long.

He pulled the bike alongside a sidewalk and kicked the stand down. As the bike tilted, Tansi adjusted herself, trying to figure out how she could get off without looking like an idiot. When she tried to get up, he gently grabbed her thigh and then held up a finger as he dismounted and offered her his hands. She took them and still stumbled onto the sidewalk, nearly twisting her ankle. She didn't want to remove the helmet and let him see her flushed embarrassment, but he was already taking his off.

"Well, this is the place," he said with a smile, motioning behind him at the sign above a small store. It read SUGARMAN'S CREAMERY, with a cartoon rendition of what she assumed was likely Sugarman: a plump man with an inviting smile who was holding a vanilla shake in his hands.

"I thought we were going for drinks?" Tansi asked, but she grinned as she held the helmet against her stomach. He retrieved her purse from the bag and handed it to her.

"I told you I only drink the good stuff," he said, then opened the door for her to pass through. A little bell jingled above their heads and startled her. The interior of the store was pure white, offset by pale mint decor and stripes. It was so bright that she wiped beneath her eyes to make sure they weren't watering.

She followed his lead as he approached the counter and surveyed the containers of ice cream in the plexiglass case. A young girl came over with her gloves on and gave them a smile of more braces than teeth.

"Any samples?" she asked.

Tansi looked at Elijah for confirmation, nerves creeping back into her gut. She couldn't pull her eyes away from his face at first as he examined the selection with bright eyes. This entire situation was so surreal.

"Oh, she wants to try the special for sure." Elijah laughed, and the girl took a little wooden spoon to scoop a tiny dollop of the ice cream on the tip. She handed it across the counter, and Elijah retrieved it and handed it to Tansi.

She took it, placing the ice cream in her mouth carefully. The taste of the wood on her tongue took her back to a childhood school cafeteria. The ice cream had hints of salted caramel and graham cracker and honey. Even after she swallowed the modest serving, her tongue and jaws tingled with pleasure.

"It doesn't get better than that, does it?" she asked, returning the satisfied grin that Elijah was giving her.

"Great, give us two of the specials. Shakes," he told the girl, retrieving his wallet.

"Singles or doubles?"

"Oh, doubles of course."

The girl took her time scooping the ice cream and blending it with milk into a creamy shake. She handed them both of the milkshakes in tall, swirled glasses across the counter, and Elijah moved to the register to pay her. Tansi wanted to take some initiative, so she took hers and sat down at a two-seat booth against the front window. She awkwardly put her helmet on the table, nervously watching as it rocked.

Elijah joined her, much more careless with his own helmet.

"Thanks for coming along," he said, taking such a forceful sip of the milkshake that his cheeks became concave.

"I needed to get out," Tansi said with a shrug. She was suddenly self-conscious about everything – her nails with chipped polish and crooked tips, the dark roots of her hair peeking through, the healing cigarette burn on her neck, the still lingering bruises beneath her eye makeup.

She tried to drive the conversation: "So, you like music? I mean... everyone likes music. I just mean... you mentioned my t-shirt."

"You don't have to be nervous," Elijah said. "We're just two people drinking the best milkshakes in Sunning. Yeah, I like music. I saw The Destroying Angels live, once."

"You did?"

"Yeah, at this place in New Ashton. Club Three, I think."

"Do you go that way much? I mean towards New Ashton."

"Not anymore. I used to travel around to a lot of bars and clubs to do performances, but you know... slave to the almighty dollar and all."

"We might've run across each other. You know, in another life. I'm from that area. I might have told you that already... Sorry, I'm rambling."

"I think I'd remember if we had been in the same room before. That night at the Flaming-O, you were the only person I saw in the whole room."

Tansi cleared her throat, heat flushing her cheeks and stomach doing an awkward flip. "It's a shame what happened to Club Three, and The Destroying Angels too."

"I knew what happened to the band. Shit is wild... I didn't hear about the club, though. Spill the tea." He winked at her.

"Child trafficking, drugs."

"No shit?"

She nodded and hummed an "mmmhm" in her throat as she drank the milkshake.

"I guess I shouldn't be surprised. That town has a really dark history with stuff like that."

He had *no* idea. Tansi wondered how he would react to hearing about the clubs that Donnie had connections to, where people paid to rape and torture women and girls— men and boys, too. No one was safe. The mere thought that these places existed and the fact that they could not be scrubbed away was terrifying and sobering. They would never run out of business because the only thing more prevalent than depravity was the amount of people willing to pay to participate in it.

"So, listen," Elijah started, "I've got this thing coming up in a couple of weeks, it's—"

The buzzing of a cell phone interrupted him, and Tansi jumped at the sensation of her purse buzzing on her thigh. She withdrew the phone and saw Alice's name across the screen.

Her finger hovered over the "decline call" button. Alice knew this was an important night for her; she wouldn't call unless it was something serious. Right?

"I, um, I think I need to take this. I'm so sorry," Tansi stammered.

"Hey, it's no big deal," Elijah remarked, stirring the bottom of his glass to loosen the last bits of milkshake.

She answered and put the phone to her ear, clearing her throat. "Alice? Everything alright?"

"No, Tansi. No, it's not alright. I need you to come right now." Alice's voice was low, as though she was afraid someone would hear her. The way her voice wavered set Tansi on edge.

"Alice, I'm in the city. I can't—"

"Tansi, please."

Tansi's eyes flicked to Elijah, who was watching her intently. She wondered if he could hear Alice's voice from the phone.

"Are *they* there?" she asked, her own voice dropping in volume.

"No."

"You swear to me?"

"I swear."

"Okay, I'll be there soon."

As she ended the call, she thought she heard Alice mutter something like, "Hurry, I can't do this by myself."

"Something wrong?" Elijah asked, brows softening into a look of concern. He wasn't mad or disappointed. He was worried. The relief Tansi felt was nauseating.

"I think so. I don't know. I'm so sorry... I have to cut this short."

"Don't apologize," he responded, getting to his feet. "Let's take you home."

She remembered the little bell when they exited to the street, the weight of the helmet on her head. She remembered the way he preemptively put the bottom of his shirt over her clasped fingers around his waist. The rest of the drive back to Jessop Terrace was a blur. She felt like she had just gotten on the back of the bike when it was already time to step off, with Elijah's help, onto the dingy sidewalk. The pink lights seemed so much harsher now, staining everything.

Elijah retrieved her purse from the saddlebag, replacing it with her helmet. She removed his jacket and handed it to him.

"I'm so sorry," she said again.

"Shit happens; there's nothing to apologize for."

She tucked her hair behind her ears and focused her eyes somewhere on the cracked sidewalk between them, gathering all of the confidence she had.

"When can I see you again?"

He grinned at her.

"I'll be back at the Flaming-O next weekend. Maybe after my performance we can just... I don't know, hang out?"

"I'd like that," she said with a soft smile.

He took a step towards her, and she caught herself tensing at the motion. He leaned in towards her, but she didn't move. She knew that in this situation, she wasn't obligated to react; she wasn't obligated to let him kiss her. But she *wanted* to. She closed her eyes, but his lips brushed her left cheek and not her mouth. Her eyes fluttered open in surprise, catching him just as he pulled away from her with a smile.

"See you next weekend, then."

Tansi waved as he put the helmet on and drove away. She stood there for several moments before she went upstairs.

She almost forgot that she had returned because Alice asked her. She thought about how she'd tell Alice about the night she'd had, the way she felt.

Then she opened the door to the apartment. She smelled the metallic tang of blood and decay before she even saw anything. It sobered her mood immediately. Alice was sitting on the bed, her eyes puffy and red. She looked twice as old as she had when Tansi left earlier in the evening.

"Alice? What's going on?" Tansi felt a lump in her throat nearly squeezing the voice out of her.

"The bathroom," Alice said without moving her eyes. They were unfixed, staring somewhere far away.

Tansi slowly walked to the bathroom door, which had been pulled almost closed but not latched. She pushed it open with her fingers and absorbed the scene. There was blood everywhere – smeared on the countertop, the floor, and on the handle and seat of the toilet. Water poured out of the overflowing toilet onto the floor, and on top of the water, a veined purple disk and something grey spun in a slow circle as the toilet attempted to drain.

Against the edge of the tub in the corner, Lucy sat in just a t-shirt. Her thighs and hands were coated in blood, and she had smears of it on her face like warpaint.

Tansi put her hands to her mouth, dropping her purse on the ground as she rushed into the bathroom, shoes squeaking across the wet floor. She fell to her knees beside Lucy, scooping her against her chest, squeezing her tightly.

"It's okay, Luce," Tansi whispered, kissing her hair. "Let's get you cleaned up okay?"

Tansi looked over her shoulder at the doorway, "Alice? I need your help."

Her words were firm and sharp, demanding. Alice appeared in the doorway but still looked dazed and dissociated. Tansi didn't want to be here either, not now, handling this. Someone had to do something.

"Get some paper towels, the mop. Whatever we have to clean with. Trash bags," Tansi instructed, reaching over to turn on the water and switch it from shower to bath. She tested the temperature on her wrist and then closed the stopper.

"C'mon, Luce," Tansi said, voice soft. She pulled Lucy's t-shirt over her head and helped her into the tub. As the girl stood, dark blood poured down her legs, leaving puddles on the floor. "Just sit here for a minute and relax, okay? We're gonna take care of all of this, alright? It'll all be okay."

Lucy didn't respond, still sobbing quietly as she sat in the water and allowed it to fill around her. Tansi closed the curtain so the girl didn't have to watch as Tansi and Alice set to work cleaning. It felt like the more they wiped and mopped, the farther the blood reached. They didn't have any gloves, so Alice used a slotted pasta fork to scoop out the tissue – and then Lucy's baby – from the toilet. It was a little longer than Tansi's hand. She could've cradled it on her forearm, and she thought it was remarkable how much it *looked* like a baby. It was a girl.

It hurt Tansi to put her into the garbage bag with the piles and piles of paper towels. She thought maybe she should clean her off and offer to let Lucy hold her, but she decided against it. She would regret that for the rest of her life.

The bathroom was finally clean but still held the lingering smell beneath the aroma of cheap cleaning supplies and vinegar. Alice retrieved an oversized t-shirt, underwear, and an entire pack of menstrual pads. She waited by the counter as Tansi pulled back the curtain.

At first, Tansi's gut wrenched, and she thought Lucy was dead. She sat with her arms draped over the edges of the tub, breathing shallow and her chin resting on her chest. The water was red and opaque, and chunks of black floated on the surface, clinging to her body like tiny leeches.

Tansi swallowed, turning her head as she reached past Lucy's leg to let the water drain. She helped Lucy up, drying her body meticulously with a towel. She was still bleeding, more than Tansi thought was normal. What was normal?

They dressed her, and Alice put a towel in the center of the bed before they eased Lucy onto it.

"Lucy, you need to go to the hospital, okay? I'm going to call an ambulance," Alice said softly.

"No," Lucy said, voice clear, "not tonight."

"Lucy," Tansi interjected, "you're bleeding."

"Not tonight."

They exchanged looks but agreed. The two girls changed into sleep clothes. Alice settled on one side of the bed and lay with her back to them. Tansi brushed Lucy's wet hair and dried the lingering droplets. She noticed the tracks and dark flesh on both arms, as well as behind her knees. She tucked the blankets around her neck so she didn't have to see it anymore.

Tansi slid under the sheets behind Lucy, wrapping her arms around her. She tucked her knees behind Lucy's, trying to ignore the active dampness that settled on her own thighs.

"Tans?" Lucy whispered.

"Get some sleep, Lucy. We'll call the ambulance to take you to the hospital first thing in the morning. I won't let you argue your way out of it. So rest up. You've got a lot of nurses and doctors to fight."

There was a pause, and then Lucy spoke again.

"Maybe I was all wrong. Maybe there aren't any good people. Maybe I'm not a good person, either. Maybe I deserve all of this." Her voice trailed off.

Tansi blinked away tears in the darkness, pulling Lucy closer to her and putting her mouth against her shoulder.

"You deserve the world, Luce. You are the best of us and, honestly, if you can't have the good things... none of us should."

"I'm glad you're here, Tansi," Lucy whispered, voice just a breathy sound that could've been the rustling of sheets.

"Me too, Luce."

Tansi didn't like how it felt like a goodbye.

FOURTEEN

THE DUSTY ORANGE OF the sun coming through the window woke Tansi early that morning, and she knew.

She knew Lucy was gone. She had been a source of heat through the night, but as Tansi rolled over and put her hand on her arm to rouse her, she felt the coolness of her flesh. She felt inanimate, like a doll still curled into a comfortable position on the bed. Her face looked tense around her mouth, and her eyes were staring forward and fixed.

Tansi was nauseous just from touching her, sitting up quickly in the bed to turn and put her head down. She breathed slowly through her lips.

"Alice." Tansi didn't recognize her voice: harsh and rasping from the tingle of bile and tears.

Alice stirred behind her, mumbling.

"Oh, God. Lucy."

Tansi forced herself to turn, watching as Alice touched Lucy's arm. Alice's eyes glistened with tears, but she retained what little color her face had. She was far less horrified than Tansi.

"You seen someone dead before?" Tansi asked quietly, balling her hand into a fist and holding it against her lips. She felt warm tears leave tacky trails down her cheeks and neck. Alice had gone from a frantic phone call – because she couldn't clean Lucy and the bathroom alone –

to someone who looked like she'd done this a million times, sobered by experience.

"Seen a few…" Alice whispered. "We got to move her before she gets stiff."

"Move her? Move her where? What are you talking about, Alice? I can't touch her. We've got to—"

"Tansi."

She stopped, chest aching and heaving with effort. It was that *everywhere, everywhere* hurt that Elijah had talked about in his set. Alice was looking at her with a soft and sympathetic gaze. She shook her head the smallest amount from left to right.

"We have to get her out of here. DJ will kill us if we get the police in The Palace. We can't do nothing else for Lucy right now. We have to take care of me and you."

"What are we going to do with her?"

"We'll set her out back by the dumpster."

"Alice, I can't. We can't leave her out there like she's trash. It might take days for someone to find her, or to care enough to report it. I already feel like shit putting that baby in the garbage!"

She cupped her hands together then in front of her like she was imagining its small form.

"I'll tell Zahid to call the cops and let them know somebody came in and said there's a body back there. They'll come get her quick. She'll get taken care of."

"What about her family?"

Alice paused.

They'd never discussed their old lives. Alice had never even asked Tansi where she was from, who cared about her, or who she had left behind. She'd probably never asked Lucy, either.

"We are her family." Alice said quietly.

Tansi didn't push it. She remained quiet for a moment, wiping the back of her hand across her cheek to capture a hot tear.

"I'm ready," she whispered.

Tansi didn't even put on her shoes. Alice checked the hallway to make sure the male neighbor wasn't loitering in the hallway. Everyone else on this floor was inactive during the day – too high to function or resting from a night of activity. When she confirmed the coast was clear, they hefted Lucy's body off of the bed.

She was already less pliable than Tansi expected but still floppy enough to be cumbersome. The side of her body that had been resting on the bed was darkened with purple and pink, like everything had settled there. Tansi didn't understand the processes of death. She thought people got stiff pretty instantly: comically frozen in the position they died in.

Together, they carried her down the stairs. It was a painstakingly slow journey, carefully moving so they didn't fall or drop her. Tansi kept her eyes on Alice, refusing to look at Lucy's face again.

Was it divine intervention— the way they didn't see a single soul as they traversed the flights of stairs, through the yellow-aged laundry area, and into the back alley with their dead friend in tow? Tansi's heart halted until they emerged in the harsh daylight, air heavy with cold humidity.

Alice and Tansi lowered Lucy against the dumpster. Tansi felt somehow heavier when she released Lucy, the weight leaving her hands and settling into her core.

"We have to lay her on her side. Like she was in the bed. Make it harder to tell we moved her," Alice said quietly, tipping Lucy onto the pavement, hand under her cheek to keep her head from hitting the ground.

Tansi rubbed her arm, body shaking with stress and tension.

"What do we do now, Alice?"

"I'll go talk to Zahid. You go back upstairs."

"I don't think I can be there right now... I don't think I can stand it. I gotta go change into some real clothes, but I ain't staying right now."

"Well, you need to be out of sight, or at least away from here, before the cops show up. Got it? I'll see you tonight."

"Got it."

"And Tansi... you might want to find DJ or Trixie, get him his money before he comes looking for it."

Selfishly, Tansi wanted to ignore what she said, although she knew she was right. Her brain was drowning beneath waves of numbness, pain rippling just below the surface and breaching with every ebb. The last thing she wanted to do was have another confrontation with DJ and his bottom bitch. The last thing she wanted to do was have to worry about protecting herself.

When she entered the apartment, her body began to shake again. She removed the oversized shirt and shorts she had slept in, startled by the sight of the pink stains on her thighs from Lucy's blood. She caught herself trying to wipe it away, only to find it was dry and set in. She kicked the clothes into the corner and rushed into the bathroom, submerging herself under the shower on the hottest setting. She had to add water to her shampoo in order to produce enough lather to wash it. It was exhausting, for some reason, to hold her arms up to massage her own scalp. She felt drained.

Tansi closed her eyes and sat with her head against the wall, allowing the water to pour across her shoulders until it ran cold. She stood there until she heard sirens outside.

She'd been in the shower for so long that she expected Alice to have returned, but as she dried off, she noted that the apartment was still quiet and empty.

"Alice?" She called her name into the silence, just to be sure.

She wasted no time getting dressed, stuffing what money she'd saved into her purse. She resisted the urge to exit from the back of the apartments, just to see if they'd taken Lucy yet. Instead she headed out the front, lighting a cigarette she found tucked deep in the crevasses of her purse.

She tried to work herself up to walking across the street to Pink Panther. During the day, it was closed to the public, but Donnie was almost always there. He had an office tucked away upstairs that overlooked Jessop Terrace. She'd never been in the office, but she knew it was Donnie's home away from home.

The sound of voices drew her attention to the alley beside The Palace. EMTs emerged with a body on a stretcher, its form jagged and pointy with rigidity beneath the white sheet. Tansi gulped so hard that she nearly swallowed her cigarette, stamping it out on the sidewalk. The nicotine suddenly turned her stomach sour.

They loaded the body into the back of an ambulance she hadn't noticed. Behind that ambulance was a familiar white car.

"Tansi, right?"

She turned to see Keistyn heading up the alleyway towards her. Despite the bright yellow of her pantsuit and jewelry, her expression was devoid of any joy. She wore the somber expression of disappointment... and sorrow. She was mourning Lucy, too.

"I don't remember giving you my name," Tansi responded, crossing her arms over her chest.

"You didn't have to."

Tansi tipped her chin upwards. "What's going on here? Somebody hurt?"

"You don't know?"

Despite the question, Keistyn's dark eyes looked straight through her. Tansi could tell that she knew she was lying.

Tansi's voice cracked as she responded. "Know what?"

"Your *friend*. Eloise Delgado. Her family called her Ellie. You all knew her as Lucy."

The words stung. Hearing Lucy's *real* name hurt even worse, even deeper.

"Yeah?" Tansi said, voice taking a raw edge that sounded as pained as she felt. She blinked twice to spread a premature tear, ensuring that it didn't run rogue down her cheek. "What about her?"

"She's dead, sweetheart. You know anything about that? About what happened to her?"

Tansi shook her head. "I don't know anything."

"It looks like she was using again, but I got reason to believe this might have something to do with her baby daddy. You know anything about him?"

"Nah, I don't know who it was."

"That girl didn't deserve this end," Kiestyn said, leaning towards her. "I want justice for her. I want to do whatever I can for her."

"She never should have come back here," Tansi whispered.

"Be careful out here. People are crazy these days."

"People have always been crazy."

"Yeah, well, three dead bodies that all reek of foul play in the last couple of weeks... that's something to worry about."

"Foul play?"

"Yeah. I know a cop that works this end of the city. He'll usually give me updates, especially on the girls that I'm trying to help."

"What were the names of the other girls?"

"Oh, they weren't girls. One was some college kid. Found him right over there." Keistyn pointed to a dark alley across the street. "Probably got robbed for his money. He was pretty loud at the club; everyone saw him flashing his platinum card and bragging about how rich his folks were. That's what I heard, anyway. He was stabbed twenty-four times, throat slit."

"That sounds personal."

"People are brutal. The other murder was definitely personal. Genital mutilation, beat to death with a blunt object, then thrown off the top of a parking garage."

"A parking garage? On the Strip?"

"Nah, a couple of blocks over. Abandoned property on the corner of Blackstock and Western."

"What's that got to do with us? The people here, I mean."

It was Keistyn's turn to cross her arms over her chest. She looked behind herself and then down the alleyway.

"I shouldn't be telling you any of this, but if it keeps you girls safe..."

"I didn't hear it from you," Tansi said.

"What?"

"I'm not going to tell anybody... but *if* anybody asks, I didn't hear nothing from you."

"Does the name Desmond Jeffreys mean anything to you?"

Of course it did.

"Yeah. He's my—" Tansi paused, giving Keistyn a knowing glance before averting her eyes. "He's my manager, and you know better than to press him. You, of all outsiders, of all people who don't belong here, *know* what he's capable of."

"Desmond Jeffreys is the man who was thrown off the garage. He's dead."

A cool splash of sensation mottled Tansi's face. She felt numb around her eyes and her mouth, eyes burning. DJ was dead?

"That's not possible," she finally said, voice quiet.

"It's true. If you wanted a chance to get out of the life... well, I'd take it now."

"You know it's more complicated than that."

"There's going to be a scramble of power, honey. Usually, the guy who takes control is even worse than the first one."

Donnie. Tansi resisted the urge to glance over her shoulder at Pink Panther, where she knew he was waiting inside. She clutched her purse tighter to her side, taking some comfort in hugging it against her.

"Think about it. Let me know if you want my help. There's life out there, and you know it. Leaving here doesn't mean you got to go back to whatever you came here running from. There's always plenty of new beginnings just waiting for you."

"Yeah, okay. Thanks. I gotta go. Take it easy, alright?" Tansi's voice shook as she backed away from Keistyn, watching as she held her ground.

"My cop friend will be around over the next week or so. Don't be surprised if he comes asking you and your roommate questions," she called after her.

"Why do the police care? Never cared about any of us before. Girls die out here every year... never been investigated."

It was Keistyn's turn to start walking away.

"She was pregnant, she delivered a baby. As far along as she was, it was probably viable. They wonder if someone stole it, or maybe Eloise sold it for drugs. Anyway, there's the prospect of that baby out there somewhere. They care more about babies than they do us. Always have, always will."

Tansi stopped to watch Keistyn's retreating form, thinking about the dead baby girl in the trash.

Fifteen

Tansi returned to the apartment and waited for Alice. Her mind had gone from not wanting to be inside the apartment at all, to feeling like it was the safest place in the world. She sat on the couch with her knees pulled up to her chest, phone lying on the cushion beside her.

There was a knock at the door that raised the hair along her spine. She got up, filled with trepidation, and began walking on the balls of her feet to mute as much sound as possible. The knock repeated just as she reached the door, peering through of the peephole. She barely caught sight of someone leaving, just the edge of their shoulder in a black leather jacket. If she hadn't seen a ponytail, she would have wondered if it was Elijah. She released relieved breath through her lips; a knock at the door shouldn't be this terrifying. Whoever it was must have realized they had the wrong apartment.

She slowly opened the door, peeking out into the empty hallway. The scent of perfume lingered, and there was a small brown box, very innocuous. It wasn't labeled, and there was no writing on it. It was meticulously taped.

She reached down and lifted it, giving it a gentle shake near her ear.

"What's that?"

Alice's voice startled her, and she dropped the box to the ground. It bounced once and then came to rest. Tansi put a hand to her heaving chest.

"Jesus, Alice."

"Hopefully nothing fragile."

Tansi bent down to pick up the package and motioned inside.

"I've got to tell you something, but we need to go inside. In case, you know... someone might be listening or something."

Alice nodded, apprehension forming creases around her eyes and lips as she followed Tansi into the apartment. She deposited the package on the island and leaned back against the countertop to face Alice. It felt like they should talk about what happened to Lucy, but Tansi knew Alice would shut that down immediately. Tansi thought the devastation would rot her from the inside out if she couldn't tell someone about it, but Alice was not going to be that person for her.

"DJ is dead."

Alice blinked at her, jaw hanging slack.

"Miss Ferrise— you know, that lady from the women's center— was outside earlier... guess she's got some cop that tells her when something goes down here, so she knew about Lucy. She told me there's been a few people turning up dead on The Strip, and now she thinks Lucy is related, somehow. She said somebody cut DJ up and dropped him off a building."

"Jesus Christ," Alice breathed, "who would do something like that?"

"DJ was a piece of shit. I bet he had a lot of enemies."

"But who would have the balls to off him? Everyone knows that if you mess with him, you mess with Donnie."

"For all we know, it might have been Donnie."

Alice huffed indignantly.

"I'm glad he's dead... but what does this mean for us?"

"I—" Alice paused, then cleared her throat. "What's in the box?"

Tansi turned around, grabbing a knife from the half-empty block to cut the tape off the top of the box.

"Have you seen that movie? The wife's head is in the box." Tansi laughed. "Were you expecting a package?"

"Not me."

The tape came loose, and the top of the box popped up gently. Pieces of crimped, shredded paper were stuffed inside for padding. Tansi reached inside, flinging paper playfully into the air.

"Maybe it's from that guy you've been seeing," Alice teased. "He's cute."

Tansi's stomach flipped at the suggestion and she began digging a little quicker. Then her hand brushed something inside. She tilted the box towards herself, brow furrowed. What was that?

She pulled it out of the box in her shaking hands. Tansi jerked her hand back, dropping it to the floor. Several pennies fell out onto the floor from within. She knew exactly what it was. It was a scrotum, and the top of it was sewn together with a little gold clasp.

She knew exactly what it was.

"What the hell is that?" Alice squealed, voice shrill and surprised. She jerked the box towards her, digging further and withdrawing a piece of folded paper. Tansi took it out of her hands so forcefully that she nearly ripped it. She began reading, walking away from Alice at the same time.

The sheet of paper bore the Koplin Grand letterhead.

Here's the coin purse you requested. You'll just have to trust me when I say that his dick was removed from his body, although I did put it back—I shoved it down his throat.

See you soon,
Missy

It was signed with a black lipstick print of Missy's full lips at the bottom. Tansi's head spun. She dropped the paper and stumbled to the couch, vomiting on the carpet. Luckily, she hadn't eaten, and her stomach could only produce the smallest amount of yellow bile.

Alice picked up the paper, and her eyes scanned it. She was trying to piece everything together, but Tansi was too disoriented with shock to explain.

"What the fuck is going on, Tansi? Who is Missy? Is that really—" Alice retched.

"She's the girl."

"What girl?"

Tansi gritted her teeth together, voice coming across a little harsher and more hateful than she intended. "The fucking woman that keeps picking me up."

"The one with all the money?"

"Yeah."

"Well, I guess you were fucking right when you said she gave you the creeps. What the fuck, Tansi? What did she mean that you *requested* this?"

"It wasn't like that, Alice. I didn't know she was really a psycho. I thought she was joking when she said she killed people."

"Who jokes about killing people, Tansi? Who does that?"

"I know you've been with clients who like to pretend, who like to roleplay. I've heard way weirder fantasies than a woman claiming to kill men. I thought it was just some kind of power play."

"So you decided to test it and asked her to kill somebody? Just to see?"

"No, I was joking. It's complicated. I had no idea she would actually kill him."

But she didn't feel bad. In fact, she was glad he was dead. She didn't care how it had happened or why it had happened.

"This is dangerous," Alice said, going over to the window to survey the street as though afraid someone might be there. "If Donnie finds out that you are somehow related to this, he's going to come down hard on us. He might kill us. We're already on thin ice, Tansi. Or what if this woman decides to kill you? Or me?"

"She only kills men... I think."

Alice held up her hands. "Wait. Let's think rationally about this. There is no way *that woman* killed DJ. Don't you think if any of us were capable of that, we'd done it already?"

Tansi was quiet.

"Someone else killed DJ. We need to calm down."

"What about the letter? What about the—" Tansi belched, bile rising in her throat again.

Alice walked over to the kitchen, picking up the little ball-sack coin purse, and dropped it into the garbage. Then, she raked all of the paper stuffing into the trash, along with the box. She tore up the letter from Missy, crumpling the shreds and throwing them on top of the rest of the trash.

"I know you don't want to, but we need to talk to Donnie and see where we stand," Alice said, tugging her short hair nervously. "We got to get ahead of this. Why are you looking at me like that?"

Tansi hadn't realized she was staring at Alice in disbelief. She blinked, quickly looking away, cheeks flushing.

"You didn't think if DJ died, we'd just be *free* from all this, did you? You didn't think, surely to God, that he's the only one who's got power

over us, did you? Think we could just go be independent contractors...
or live happily ever after? *That's not how this works*."

Tansi set her jaw, leaning over her own knees to stare at the floor
beneath her feet.

"I wish I never come here," she whispered.

Alice scoffed, "Yeah, well, you did."

Sixteen

Tansi thought it was about time to stop wallowing in self-pity. She knew she had pissed off Alice – and maybe betrayed her trust a little – when she didn't come back to the apartment after talking to Donnie. Tansi had texted her multiple times, with no response. She didn't blame her, really. It did look like Tansi had ordered DJ killed and while he probably deserved it... there was always someone worse in line.

She hadn't worked over the past few days, waiting for the ball to drop, but nothing happened. The fridge was empty, cabinets running low. She was going to have to get out soon, with or without Alice. Night was falling outside, and the streets came alive with vehicles and bodies.

She peeked out the window and saw the lights on at the Flaming-O. People were already heading inside.

Tansi dressed, giving Alice one more call on speaker. It went to voice-mail.

"Hey, Alice, it's me again. Just haven't heard from you and wanted to check in. Isn't like you to be gone for so long. Just shoot me a message or something, and give me some proof of life, okay? I don't care if you're on a bender or whatever... just want to make sure you're earthside. I'll be gone tonight; Elijah's performing at The Flamingo. See you soon, maybe."

She hung up and dropped her phone into her pocket. On the way to the door, she paused, backtracking to the bathroom, where she looked at herself in the mirror. As she stared at her reflection, she realized she was looking at herself in a way she wasn't used to. She was looking for something else, and she didn't know what it was. She frowned and hoisted her purse strap higher on her shoulder as she started to leave. A speck of blood they had missed on the grout caught her eye, and she couldn't look away from it. She pictured the room covered in blood like a scene from a horror movie – one of those where you snorted at the screen and said, "*There's not that much blood in a person. So unrealistic.*"

Except it had been real. The floor looked so clean now, the tile returned to its new white splendor.

She sniffled and left the bathroom, and then the apartment. Her heart leapt in her chest as she crossed the street towards the Flaming-O. She couldn't remember the last time she was this happy, this giddy. The guy at the door recognized her and nodded.

"Do you want a beer ticket?" he asked, extending a piece of paper in his hand.

She started to reach for it but then retracted her hand.

"Actually, no thank you. I don't think I'm going to drink tonight."

He nodded and let her pass through. She noticed that almost everyone wore black t-shirts, and a majority of the crowd were garbed in black, head-to-toe. There were more people than usual, too. The little speakeasy was always busy, but tonight, it was slammed. She sidled up to the bar, finding her regular bartender there.

"You again," she teased.

They gave her a crooked grin. "Yep."

"You live here, don't you?"

"Wouldn't you?"

She laughed and gestured to the people milling around the room, "Is there some kind of event going on? Or something?"

They looked her up and down and cringed. "You didn't know? The local cover band, Luminous Soul, is doing a glow party. Everyone is going to be covered in phosphorescent paint by the end of the night. I hope you don't mind possibly ruining your outfit..."

Tansi had worn another black band t-shirt and a pair of her nicest jeans. She'd dug through drawers trying to find these exact articles of clothing. Although they weren't dressy clothes, she hadn't exactly planned on getting covered in glowing paint...

"It's fine," she said with a smile. "Sounds like fun."

"Can I get you anything to drink?"

"How about a Coke?"

The corners of the bartender's lips tugged up gently and they nodded once. "You like cherries?"

"Sure."

The first performer approached the mic and started speaking. Tansi watched them until she heard the bartender slide the glass of soda across the counter behind her. Two red cherries floated in the dark liquid, leaving a film of sweetness across the top.

"On the house."

"You're too kind. You know, you're my favorite bartender here for a reason."

They laughed, walking away to serve another patron.

Tansi found herself growing more and more nervous as each performer that wasn't Elijah came onto the stage. It was a good kind of nervous, even though it made her shift in her seat with every wrenching ache of her gut. Then, when he finally came onto the stage— there were the butterflies.

Her hands were as sweaty as the glass she held. He stood quietly, pushing his mess of dark hair off of his forehead as he scanned the crowd, giving her the softest smile when his eyes finally found her. She raised a hand awkwardly and then quickly put it down.

"We are all wrapped in tragedy. It's the human condition. We need those little moments of wilting: cigarettes after sex, stopping to listen to sad songs on the radio, when we've loved and been hurt... we choose to try love again. But then, the irony— the irony that we are so afraid of giving into the wildness and lunacy that every fiber of our being craves. When you find your crazy, everything feels right. But we worry about the details. What will people think of us? The black-and-white, pressed and ironed, clean-faced people. The people who compare their glasses to ours and say, 'Mine is half full, and yours is half empty,' when it's all the same in the end. It's filled with poison and one sip will kill us anyway. Slow, tiny deaths every day. They'll run from it, deny it, wear tomes of immortality when the decades we're giving are *nothing* compared to whatever comes afterwards. Why do they hold on so tight to such a temporary thing?

"Do you run? Or do you brush fingers with It, feel that caress, and tell It you'll be right back? Just another minute, another hour, another year. Then, when It says, 'We really have to go now,' you can part like friends who have overstayed at the party. Sun's coming up, last call. You can tell It you have other arrangements, but It'll insist.

"Find that madness, the mania that makes this shit show worth it. When it's time to get into that black car to leave at the end of the day – whatever it is that makes you smile as you pull away. Time well spent.

"If they ask what drove me mad, I will tell them it was being touched by love. Like grabbing a live wire. My heart knew from the moment I was born that meeting her would fuck me up. I've seen her all my life in every beautiful thing, so I recognized her soul the moment I felt it. If I died right now, I would be okay with that. I have drunk from the sweet, burning liquor in the cup of madness, and I'm ready; I'm sated. Are you?"

Tansi's heart pounded in her chest as Elijah left the stage. Her hands were shaking so much that she turned to set the drink on the countertop. She thought if she watched his approach, she would drop the glass to the floor. The bartender supplied another Coke, and Elijah slid into the seat beside her. She cupped her drink in her hands and felt him lean just close enough that she could feel the heat of his body on her arm.

He glanced at her glass and then smiled, looking down at his own. He noticed she'd ordered the soda. She thought she could see the slightest tinge of warmth rise in the olive tone of his cheeks.

"Hey," he said, taking a sip of his drink and looking straight ahead.

"Hey."

Behind them, she could hear the band getting ready on stage, tuning their instruments and unloading everything. She felt the crowd press forward excitedly, leaving the two of them there in their own little world at the bar.

"Was everything okay?" he asked. "The other day. It drove me crazy not knowing."

He leaned over and took a pen off of a signed receipt, writing on his damp napkin. He struggled, tearing the paper more than once but diligently working before he slid it across the counter to her.

"Here's my number, if you want it. I won't be sitting awake all night beside my phone or anything..." He smiled with those stupid dimples, and Tansi thought she couldn't resist the urge to pinch his cheeks.

"Where's the nearest garbage can?" she asked, voice quiet as she feigned looking around.

He laughed, and she found herself smiling at him before she folded the paper gently and put it into her pocket.

"A friend died," she admitted, surprising herself.

"Oh, my God," Elijah breathed. "What happened? I'm so sorry."

He extended his hand across the bartop towards her hand, fingers down against the wood surface. She watched his hand but didn't close the space between them.

She couldn't tell him everything. She couldn't give him all of the details, the entire truth. No yet. She couldn't risk scaring him away, ruining the only good thing she had right now. It already felt like something she was grappling for a hold on.

"Overdosed, we think. She got messed up with the wrong people.... She was pregnant, and she wanted to do good by that baby but just made bad decisions. One too many." She reached up and frantically wiped away a tear that she almost didn't catch.

"Are you okay?" he asked. "I can't imagine how hard this must be."

"No." Her voice was so quiet that she wasn't even sure he could hear her. She moved her hand towards his until they touched; he grasped just her fingers in his and gave it a gentle squeeze.

She wanted to tell him how terrible it was. She wanted to tell him about all of the blood, about the dead baby, about the way it happened in her apartment. She wanted to tell him about what DJ, AJ, and Donnie had done to her and to Alice. She needed to tell him, but she couldn't.

The crowd behind them jeered as music started playing. A loud pop startled Tansi enough that she jumped, jerking her hand away from Elijah's. She turned around to see the bassist spraying the crowd with splatters of paint from what looked like a large party popper.

"Want to go have some fun?" Elijah asked, motioning to the stage. "They do pretty good covers."

"Yeah," she responded, "let's go."

He stood up, offering his hand to her. She took it, trying to hide her reluctance – not because she didn't want to, but because she was afraid her knees would be too weak for her to walk across the floor.

He guided her into the mass of bodies just as another spray of paint went through the crowd and the lights dimmed. Tansi squeaked in surprise and flinched as it covered her face and chest in glowing green and orange speckles.

Elijah laughed. She looked over at him in the dark, hair and nose dotted with paint. The music swelled around them, and the crowd was alive with movement. They were gently jostled as the people swayed with the music.

They *were* good.

The second song was much more upbeat, and she was knocked into Elijah more than once. He put his arm around her to hold her steady, singing along with the song as it played. She wanted to curl into him, closing her eyes as she relished the moment and mouthed the words.

The next song came on, and she felt a hand on her chin. She opened her eyes to see Elijah gazing at her, gently moving her face to look her in the eye.

His brows were furrowed with concern. He tried to yell over the sound of the music, "Are you okay?"

She took a breath to say something, forcing a smile. She was overwhelmed.

"I just—"

Shaking her head, she pulled away from him, pushing through the crowd to the bathroom. It was an all-gender bathroom with multiple stalls. She avoided the gaze of someone exiting as she went in, going to the sink and leaning over it. She shifted her purse strap across her neck to make it more difficult to fall off as a crossbody.

"What are you doing here?" Tansi whispered to herself, searching the eyes of the paint-covered girl in the mirror.

The door opened, music clear and loud for just a moment. She turned to see Elijah standing there. He moved to the side, as though he was afraid to block the door in case she wanted to leave.

"Is everything okay?" he asked again.

"Yeah. I think I may just go home for the night."

She hated herself for saying it and wanted to take it back immediately. Attempting to backtrack, she mumbled, "I mean, I don't know. I don't know what I want; what I need."

"Did I do something that bothered you? Offended you? I'm sorry if I overstepped your boundaries or something."

"No," she said, taking a step towards him. "You didn't do anything wrong. You're fine. You're perfect. Honestly, maybe too perfect. Too good for me."

She saw a confused look on his face, lips parted as though he was also searching for the right words.

Oh *God*. She had misread this entire thing. He didn't like her *like that,* and she'd just made an assumption and now this was awkward. How conceited and naive did she have to be to assume that he liked her after such a short time and that he would do some spoken word thing about her? Stupid, stupid, stupid. She felt her cheeks flush and cleared her throat.

"I am so sorry. I am such a dumbass to assume that you wanted to... I mean that you could possibly even be interested in someone like—"

"Tansi," he interrupted her. For some reason, the sound of that name on his lips made her cringe. She wanted him to call her by her real name, but did that girl even exist anymore? She was more of a persona than Tansi was.

He stepped towards her and cupped her face in his hands. She didn't know for sure who initiated the kiss that followed; it felt like they just fell into each other.

The interior of the bathroom was both deafening and silent. As he pressed her against the cold tile, she could feel the bass of the music pulsing through the walls. She heard him flip the lock on the door as his mouth moved to her neck, his hands on her hips. She marveled at how his touch made it feel like her flesh fell away and she was left with naked nerves that burst to life with every caress. This was different, so different. She had never felt anything like this before. She tattooed every sensation and detail into her brain. The muffled sound of the song would be *their* song in her head from then on. Not the way it sounded on the radio, but the new song it became at the distance beyond the walls of the bar: muffled and muted.

As someone began banging on the locked door, the thudding became one with the rhythm of her heart. They didn't relent, yelling into the crack of the door that they needed in.

Elijah pulled away, and she found herself panting like he had pulled the breath from her. He pressed his forehead against hers, wrapping his arms around her to kiss her one more time.

She had never seen anyone look at her the way he was looking at her in that moment.

"Are you in love with me yet?" he asked, grinning.

She tried to stifle her own smile, but she could almost feel the excited glint in her eyes. She stood on her tiptoes to try to reach his lips but only grazed them. "Go to hell."

He pulled her away from the door, flipping the lock open.

"Meet me there?"

Seventeen

Another morning came, and Alice still hadn't been back to the apartment. Tansi had sat up part of the night waiting on her. She wanted to tell her about Elijah and the way she felt and the way she thought that maybe he felt.

She checked her phone again, but there was no response from Alice.

"Oh, shit," she said aloud, crawling to the end of the bed to retrieve her pants from the night before. She dug out the wadded napkin and typed in Elijah's number with shaking fingers. She sent a text to him, just the single word: *Hey*.

For a brief moment she worried that maybe it wasn't really his number, or maybe she should tell him who she was because of course he didn't have her number... but almost instantly, she saw the bouncing dots of a pending reply. She wadded her comforter in her fist, pressing it against her top teeth.

I know I said I wouldn't wait all night, but here I am more coffee than human.

sorry who is this?

Whoever you want it to be.

lol cheesy

When can I see you again?

I have some things i have to get straightened out
but hopefully soon, im sorry i just haev to deal
with some things

I'm happy to take all the time I need to figure you
out. I wasn't joking about the sleep… Going to
power nap before work. Don't keep me up again
tonight </3

Tansi was the happiest she had been in as long as she could remember.
She was hopeful and optimistic, a feeling so foreign that she didn't know
how to handle it. She stared down at the phone in her hands, overcome
by the impulse to scroll through her contacts, and fixated on "MOM."

Her heart hammered in her throat as she took a deep breath. She
hadn't talked to her mother in what felt like a lifetime. She had just left.
Guilt crept in. What was it that made her want to reach out now?

"I can't believe I'm doing this."

Tansi delayed as long as possible, leaving her mom's contact info open
on the screen. She showered, scrubbing off the paint from the night before. She brushed her teeth. She dressed. One task, another task, another.
She even cleaned the apartment and walked to the convenience store to

buy a few items, biding her time until the club opened so she could go talk to Donnie. She just needed to take her time...

When Tansi entered the apartment again, she was eating the last few bites of a premade sandwich and sucking mostly air through the straw of a polished-off fountain drink. Painstakingly, she shelved the few groceries she managed to purchase, and then all that remained were the growing dark outside and the phone.

She punched the number and put it to her ear, closing her eyes as it rang and rang. She thought she might not answer at first, as the tone droned on in her ear. After leaving home, she got a new number, turning off the phone that her mother and father had been paying for. Although resolute in her abandonment of her old life, she still added those old phone numbers to her contact list when she got the new phone, just in case.

"Hello?"

Tansi jerked, eyes snapping open. She stared at the wall as she absorbed the voice on the other end.

In the silence, the voice repeated, "Hello? Can you hear me?"

"Hey, Mom," Tansi choked out, and she realized she was crying. "It's me."

Her mother audibly gasped, the violent inhale ending with a sound full of so much pain that it felt like a knife to Tansi's heart.

"Charlie?"

The use of her nickname could have been a mortal wound. She closed her eyes tightly.

"Honey, are you still there? Please don't hang up. Please say something, please," her mother begged, sobbed.

"I'm here."

"Where are you? We have been so worried about you. We haven't went a single day without looking for you."

"I can't tell you where I am right now. I just wanted to let you know that I'm okay. I just wanted... I just wanted to let you both know that I love you and that I'm sorry. I'm sorry that I hurt you."

"We just want you to come home. We'll do anything to bring you home. Please tell me what you need me to do. Your father is getting his shoes on right now."

Tansi could hear her mom snapping her fingers and her dad stumbling around, no doubt trying to put on his boots while standing on a single foot. The image almost made her smile.

"I can't come home. I've made some really bad decisions, some things I know I can't undo... but I'm here. I'm alive. I love you."

"Charlie, please."

"I love you, Mom. Please tell Dad I love him too. I'm sorry. I'm going to hang up now. Maybe I'll talk to you soon.... Please don't try to call back."

Her mother repeated her name, the hysteria rising in her voice.

"What's going on? What's she saying? Let me talk to her." She heard her father's voice in the background.

Tansi hung up the phone, letting it fall to the counter as she rubbed her eyes and sniffled. The phone immediately rang, Her mom's name flashing across the screen. Tansi declined the call and blocked the number.

Back to real life. She shoved down the pain that hurt *everywhere, everywhere.* It was dangerous to let it bloom into regret.

Tansi crossed the street, talking herself through her nerves and how she would approach the situation with Donnie. She needed to act like she didn't suspect anything crazy. She needed to ask the right questions and get out.

"Hey."

Tansi stopped in her tracks. She could recognize that voice anywhere. She didn't have to turn around; she could pretend she hadn't heard her. Pretend that Missy's voice hadn't carried as clear as day over the sound of the car engine.

But she was desperate for money, and she was desperate for answers.

Tansi turned slowly, walking over to the open window and peering into the dark vehicle.

"Got time?" Missy asked.

"I have to do something in Panther; it won't take me long. Just wait right here, and I'll take care of you."

"We're going to my place. I've got the money. I'll be here."

Missy rolled up the window and shut off the headlights.

Tansi headed into the Pink Panther, jumping the line and sliding in behind the bouncer. As usual, the club was already full of people. A man in a tight black shirt approached her once she was inside. She recognized him as one of the security guards.

"You looking for Donnie?" he asked.

Tansi nodded and followed him up the stairs, as though she didn't know where Donnie's office was. He rapped his knuckles on the room, a corner office of sorts. Donnie permitted entry from the other side, and the guard opened the door.

"Tansi, baby," Donnie exclaimed, beaming at her. He held his arms out wide as though welcoming her to his domain. "To what do I owe this pleasure?"

"Hey, Donnie," Tansi said, stepping cautiously into the office. The door was shut behind her. She stole a glance at her feet. The floor of the office was made of glass, and below her shoes was one of the many private rooms that men booked for whatever despicable needs they thought they had.

"Have a seat. I've been wondering about you." Donnie closed a book on his desk, one that looked like it might be a ledger.

She stepped forward with that same hesitation, watching between her feet as two men circled a bound woman on a chaise lounge, like sharks. She wondered if it was consensual as she set her eyes on Donnie and settled into the chair.

"I've been laying low," Tansi started. "I tried to find DJ, but no luck. Trixie avoided us. Then I heard somebody offed DJ over on Blackstock and Western."

"Where'd you hear about it?" Donnie asked suspiciously.

"Overheard somebody talking about it. Lucy's dead. They come and picked her body up, were talking about a couple of other deaths, and DJ's name came up."

Donnie didn't seem totally convinced.

"Me and Alice was just wondering where we stand, what we need to do. I thought Alice was coming to talk to you, but I haven't seen her in days. Starting to get a little worried about her."

"It's a shame about Lucy," Donnie said and despite the way his voice sounded sympathetic, he wore a shit-eating grin.

Tansi sat up straighter in her seat and cleared her throat, refusing to show any vulnerability. She didn't want to give him the satisfaction.

"Not sure what happened with DJ," he went on. "The man had a lot of enemies, and he wasn't exactly the sharpest tool in the shed. Honestly surprised this didn't happen sooner. But don't worry; I'm going to take care of you girls. I'll run some numbers, and we'll talk about my cut, get you on a schedule. I want all of you to do a little work in the club. Don't worry, nothing too intense. I just got a *lot* of clients, and I need a lot more girls. You'll be popular."

The way he looked at her was hungry. He might as well have been salivating on his desk.

"So, about Alice."

"Alice. Yeah, you know... I haven't talked to her in a while either. Probably not since DJ disappeared. Actually, I don't think I've seen her since that day at your apartment."

"She said she was coming here to talk to you," Tansi insisted, voice shaking.

"What can I say, Tansi? Maybe she decided to get out of town since DJ was out of the picture. Skip out on her debt while she could. Greener pastures."

Alice would never leave the Strip; she didn't believe there was anything left for them in the world. Even if she did, she would never have left Tansi.

"Okay. I just wanted to know if you'd seen her. I gotta go. Client waiting for me outside."

"I'll be in touch. Oh, and Tansi? Be careful out there. We just never know when our time is up."

Tansi didn't want to think about what he might mean by that. She rushed out of the office, striding across the catwalk and down the stairs. She looked over her shoulder more than once, even when she was back out on the street. She was relieved to find Missy's car still parked. She never thought she would be *happy* to see that crazy bitch.

She went directly to the passenger side and got inside, taking a deep breath.

"Another fun visit?" Missy asked, pulling onto the road.

Tansi didn't respond, staring out the window as the car took the now familiar path to the Koplin Grand.

"I'll only be in town for a little longer," Missy said. "I'll be seeing you a few more times between now and then."

"You know... I got a question. What's a girl like you calling on girls like me for, anyway?"

Missy regarded her cooly, eyes narrowing before she turned her attention back to the highway.

"You know I have to ask. You aren't my usual clientele. Seems like a girl like you would be looking for something... a little more permanent."

The other woman cringed – the most evident display of disgust Tansi had seen from her. "I just want to get fucked."

Tansi huffed a "woof" and then sighed. "Well, you got the money, and I got the *fucking* covered."

"Good."

Tansi couldn't gather the courage to ask about DJ, not yet. Maybe after they'd had sex, or whatever it was that she wanted tonight. Maybe Missy would be less intense during the comedown. The rest of the drive was a bit of a haze, Tansi dissociating to the point that she didn't even remember parking and getting out of the car. She didn't remember going up to the room or taking off her clothes. She thought about where Alice might be; she thought about Lucy and how she must have felt in the last hours of her life, the way Tansi's mother sobbed on the phone, and more than anything, she thought about Elijah.

She jolted back to the present as the waves of an orgasm unwound in her core, clutching Missy's thigh as it rested across her stomach with enough pressure that flesh peaked between the indentions that her fingers made.

She wondered if Missy would kill her too, but she reminded herself of the theory she had told Alice before: Missy maybe only killed men. Maybe.

She seemed satisfied, not moving from their tangled position on the bed. Tansi reached down, just for good measure, and slid her middle finger across her moist and swollen clit. Missy shuddered and moved away from her, propping herself up on her elbow as she continued to rest on the bed perpendicular to Tansi.

It was now or never.

"So... did you kill him? DJ. The guy."

She thought it was better to be straight with her, as she imagined dancing around the topic would only piss Missy off.

Missy looked at her, but Tansi couldn't tell if she was angry or surprised or glad she asked. She just *looked* at her, and then she sat up slowly, crawling towards her and pressing her knees apart to climb between her legs. She put her hands on either side of Tansi, hovering over her body as she regarded her with that inanimate expression. Something beyond animalistic, but still predatory. Unnatural and unsettling.

Her hair fell around them and made her face appear even darker, eyes so indistinct in the dimness that Tansi swore they were reflective and slitted like a cat's.

"That's what you wanted me to do, wasn't it? More than... anything in the world, you said?"

One of Missy's hands traveled up Tansi's thighs, slipping between her legs, fingers curling inside, gently. Tansi tensed as the tips of Missy's nails grazed her sensitive skin.

"I didn't know you..."

"Didn't know what?" Missy cooed, putting her fingers between her lips and sucking their combined flavors from her fingertips.

"That you were really killing people."

"I told you I did. I confessed to you."

"But..."

"Your disbelief is not my problem. Do you want me to tell you how I did it?" She traced her hand up Tansi's sternum, and the closer it came to her throat, the more tense she became.

"N-no," she stammered, trying to relax. She felt like Missy was feeding on her fear, hungrily consuming every ounce of discomfort and intimidation. Then the woman's fingers were around her neck. It was just one handed, but the pressure was consistent. Tansi felt herself breathing more quickly, mouth dry, eyes watering.

"It was so easy. He went with me willingly, and then I beat him to death. I didn't want to touch his disgusting dick, but I did. I did that for you. I cut it off and pried his jaws open. They were locked up pretty tightly, but I used my knife and cut here—" she moved her hand up Tansi's throat to rest tightly under her chin, index and middle fingers pressing against the left hinge of her jaw, thumb adding pressure to the right, "—sliced that open, dug around in that joint, and it went pretty slack. Then I shoved his dick down his own throat. I did that for you."

Tansi was nauseous. She pursed her lips together tightly to attempt to quell the sensation.

Missy shook her once, squeezing her throat tighter. "I think I deserve some gratitude for doing what no one else has been willing to do for you."

"Thank you. Thank you," Tansi squeaked, and she felt tears run into her hair and around the curves of her ears.

"I'm not done, either. Don't you worry... I've made a list. Those other wastes of space? It's only a matter of time. The clock is ticking. I try to be patient but... fuck is it hard to resist."

As she pressed her body against Tansi's, she couldn't hold back the queasiness any longer. She felt herself vomit in her mouth, throat fighting against the pressure of Missy's fingers. It flooded her throat, and she tried to turn her head to the side as it frothed from her lips. Missy didn't seem to be disgusted or surprised. She tipped Tansi's head up, pressing her head further into the mattress. Tansi had the sudden sensation of drowning, choking. She grabbed Missy's wrist and coughed, a sudden burst of air from her mouth as she tried not to inhale or swallow the vomitus. It forced it out of her nose and the sides of her mouth.

Missy released her, leaving her lying on the bed as she moved over to her dresser to retrieve a pair of silk panties. Tansi rolled onto her stomach, heaving what vomit remained onto the comforter and gasping for air. She didn't dare say anything.

"Go get yourself cleaned up. I think we're done here for now." Missy forcefully tossed Tansi's clothes at her, hitting her in the face. "Oh, and here... this is yours. What was it you said... if I've got the money, you've got the fucking, right?"

She tossed a wallet onto the bed, and Tansi stared down at it. It was made of an olive drab canvas, stained dark with what she thought — no, what she knew — was blood.

"Open it, see if you're satisfied." Missy commanded.

Tansi opened the wallet and saw DJ's face staring back at her from his driver's license. There were business cards, credit cards, and at least a dozen hundred dollar bills.

Tansi was terrified. It was hard to wrap her mind around the now confirmed fact that this woman was a murderer. Not just a murderer, but a serial killer.

She risked a glance up at the gorgeous woman who now stood, fastening her bra.

"Good. We wouldn't want to have a disagreement," Missy said, and she winked.

She scared the hell out of her.

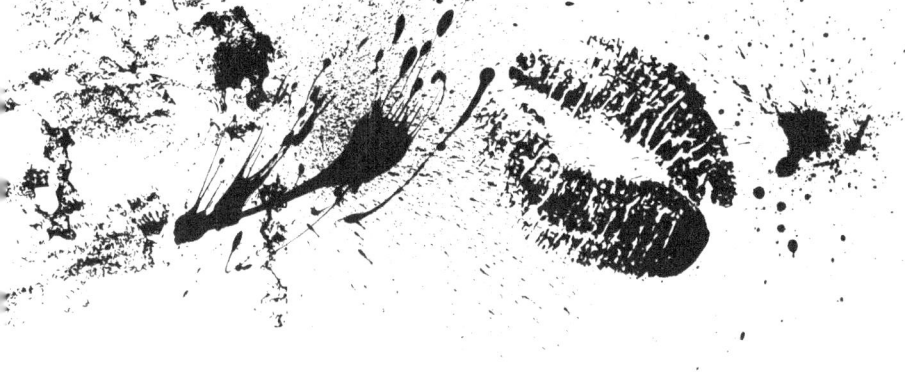

Aaron hadn't originally been on Missy's hitlist, but the way that he was so *fearful* had her chomping at the bit.

She wanted to see the look in his eyes when he realized she'd been the one who killed DJ, and now, she was going to kill him too. She wanted to watch him die, but more than that, she wanted to watch as he ceased to live.

She had followed him home a few times to scope out the area. This house was one of maybe a dozen just barely set apart from the main portion of The Strip. They were all the same: low to the ground with dirty, overgrown yards, and filled with people who minded their own business. She liked people who minded their own business. This apathy made everything so much easier for her.

Tonight was the night. She noted that he seemed particularly unsettled this evening. A twitchy and paranoid body language usually suggested the person was doing drugs, but Missy wasn't convinced that drug abuse was what was going on with Aaron. So she started tailing him from Pink Panther, where he had no doubt talked to the club owner and been given a task. She was cautious at first, concerned that someone would show up at the house, but as night drew on, it was clear that no one was coming. She lingered in the area for a little while and then slunk to the vehicle in his driveway.

Missy was pleasantly surprised to find the car door unlocked. She would never fail to be surprised by the stupidity and trust of people. Maybe it was conceit: believing that his connections would protect him from every creeping thing in the dark.

As she popped open the door and sat inside, dogs barked from the back of the house. She hesitated for a moment, dark eyes watching the windows for signs that someone was going to check to see what they were barking at.

She fucking hated animals.

The sound of a back door opening had her freezing again, motionless. She heard a man's voice as he screamed at the chained dogs.

"Shut the *fuck* up!"

This only caused the dogs to bark louder, but she resumed digging through the center console. There wasn't a wallet in the car – no surprise there. Women sometimes left their purses, with all of the contents, on the passenger floorboard, but men usually kept their wallets tucked away in their pockets.

She didn't *really* need it; it just would have made things more simple. She popped open the glove box and pulled out the registration for the vehicle, her eyes scanning the name and confirming that this was Aaron, cousin of DJ. She had listened to enough gossip inside that disgusting strip club to know that Aaron, sometimes called AJ, was on edge since his more infamous cousin had shown up dead. She knew enough from the gossip and eavesdropping to determine a few details about Aaron, but the most important thing was he was walking on thin ice with both DJ and Donnie. He was desperate, and he was soft. This was the type of guy who did what he was told like a good little pawn.

She shoved the registration back into the glove box and saw something shiny in the dark drawer: a gun. Missy retrieved a pair of leather gloves from her pocket and withdrew the gun, releasing the magazine against her palm. It was loaded. She smirked, tucking it into the pocket of her leather jacket.

She took the car key that sat in the cupholder and shut the car door quietly. She crept to the side of the house, disappearing into the shadow of an old refrigerator as she pressed the panic button on the key.

The car screamed to life, horn wailing into the night, lights flashing. The dogs barked even louder, and what sounded like hundreds more joined them throughout the neighborhood. The screen door at the front of the house swung open violently, and Aaron rushed out the door with the phone tucked between his shoulder and ear. Missy noted that it looked like he had blood on his white wife beater.

Now, now, now... what was he up to? This boy wasn't a killer; even this early, Missy could tell that he didn't have it in him.

"Hang on, my fucking car is going off..." Aaron barked into the phone, slinging his door open and getting inside.

"I'm trying, I can't find my key. Christ. You know what, I'll just..."

Missy watched as he pulled the latch on the front of the car and struggled with the hood. She took the opportunity to move with a quick confidence into the house, not bothering to stop the slamming screen door behind her.

She hoped he would notice the noise, but he didn't react if he did. She peered through a sheer curtain that hung over the front window as Aaron unplugged the battery of the car and continued talking. He reached into his pocket and withdrew a joint, lighting it and pacing up and down the driveway as he talked and smoked.

Missy detected a familiar odor inside the house and slowly followed her nose down the small entry hall and into the kitchen. She kept her eyes on the floor, searching for the body that she knew had to be lying somewhere inside. Her boots made a sticky noise on the linoleum as the hallway widened into the kitchen.

A low rumble alerted her to a dog.

Two. Fucking. Dogs.

She relaxed her body language when she realized the animals were at least somewhat contained, meeting their gaze directly as they stared at her from behind a baby gate inside what seemed to be a laundry room. Their faces were covered in blood, and there were pieces of sinew and tissue on the floor around their feet. The dogs were thin with prominent spines and slim forms that didn't match their massive heads.

Missy made a small kissing noise at them, and their tails wagged apprehensively. She pursed her lips together in grim satisfaction. They were stupid, but not territorial or aggressive. She surveyed the rest of the kitchen. Against the back door sat several large buckets from a local home improvement store. The floor around the buckets was speckled with blood. She approached the containers, kicking one of them gently with her foot.

A soupy mess lay inside with hands and feet amid chunks of other body parts. One bucket contained only a head.

Curiosity killed the cat.

Missy reached down to grasp the short, damp hair and flipped the head over before dropping it back down so she could see it. Her eyes narrowed as she peered into the pale, blood-soaked face. The eyes were wide open, the lips were torn and bloodied, and every tooth had been pried from her gums.

She recognized the head. It was the woman that lived with Tansi in that shitty apartment: the older lady. She usually wore a wig, but it was definitely her.

Missy raised a brow and looked back at the front door. Someone had been very naughty.

Tools were scattered in the sink, and on the counter lay several personal effects, including a crucifix necklace. It was the only thing that seemed like it might have been special to the dead woman. Missy took it in her hand and then dropped it into her pocket.

The sound of Aaron's voice grew louder, and she heard his feet on the steps leading into the house. She slipped into a small room just off of the kitchen, a pantry of sorts, leaving the door open only enough that she could survey the tiniest sliver of the room. The dogs looked straight at her, and she swore she'd cut *them* up into pieces if they gave her away prematurely. She withdrew the gun from her pocket and waited. She wasn't very prepared, but the gun was a godsend. She had a bunch of zip ties, and her knife.... She could improvise.

Aaron stormed into the kitchen. He tossed his phone onto the small table, lacing his hands behind his head as he hissed between his teeth and turned around in the room. It gave her a good view of his waistband, and she noted no other weapon.

He was crying. She soaked up the overwhelmed redness of his face, the way he cringed with his entire body and shook with terror. He didn't want to be here. He didn't want to do any of this.

Yet, still he did it. He could not *help* but do it.

He lifted one of the dogs effortlessly over the baby gate, setting it on the floor as he tried to feed it another body part from the bucket. The dog chewed the chunk excitedly, tail wagging.

"Eat it faster, please, you stupid fucking dog," Aaron pleaded, still crying. "You have to be hungry. I haven't fed you in days. Please just eat it. There's so much... so much."

The other dog clawed at the baby gate, seemingly unaware that it could just jump over it if it wanted.

"I can't do this," Aaron whispered, and he disappeared out of sight.

Missy perked up, trying to listen to his footsteps. He went to the right, into a room she hadn't been in yet. She thought she had glimpsed a television and a couch. Her suspicions were confirmed as she heard the TV flip on. She made eye contact with the dog through the crack in the door as it chewed the last pieces of the meat.

She pressed the door open slowly, and the dog didn't react to her. Satisfied, she ignored it and walked into the living room.

Maybe it was the way she was unflinching and unhesitating, striding in like she owned the house. Maybe it was because Aaron was at the end of his rope and – deep down – *wanted* this. Whatever the reason, Aaron didn't get up from the small sofa. His jaw dropped when Missy came to stand between him and the television, but he didn't try to move. He just... sat there.

"Hey, who the—"

The safety clicked off, and the next sound was the gun firing. The dogs' nails skittered across the tile floor in surprise, and they both started barking. A delayed wail peeled from Aaron's lungs, a sound more suited for a child than a grown man. He howled into the air, head slung backwards.

Missy held the end of the gun under her nose, inhaling with a sigh. "I love the smell. I don't get the opportunity to use a gun often enough. Too many things can go wrong; too many things can lead back to you. Just messy."

She glanced at the kitchen and then returned her focus to him "You know all about messy, though, don't you?"

She stalked towards Aaron as he clutched at his bleeding crotch, a purple flower blossoming against the denim. He threw his head back again, teeth gritted, and she thought he might have an aneurysm before she even got to play with him.

"Oh, did I do that?" she chirped, pouting at him.

He was hyperventilating, both hands pressed against his wound. The way he wasn't trying to get away or fight her off was both infuriating and provoking.

"Let me see," she said.

He shook his head. "Who are you?"

"I said..." –she pointed the gun at his face, touching the barrel to his temple– "let me see. Pull your pants down."

"Please, I don't know what you want. I think you might be in the wrong house. I've never seen you before in my life."

"Aaron, sweetie," she said, feigning amusement. "Don't try to rationalize this. What do I want? I want you to pull your pants down, or I'm going to shoot you in your face. How's that?"

"But why?" he whispered.

She whispered back, "I'm going to look at your balls or brains. Three seconds... two seconds..."

He breathed the word "okay" and unbuttoned his pants with shaking hands. He didn't try to stand up, shimmying his hips until he slid the pants and his pair of plaid boxers down around his knees.

Aaron stared down at his groin: the cartridge had gone through his dick and torn open his left testicle before resting somewhere in the couch cushion beneath him. A gray and purple testicle was peeking through, slipping in and out of the gash with every breath he took.

"Oh, tsk, tsk," Missy said.

"Please, just let me go to the hospital. I won't tell anybody you were here. I don't even know who you are. I don't understand what you want."

The dog from the kitchen padded in, nervously leaning towards Aaron's wounded penis.

Missy twirled the gun.

"Turn around. I'm going to bind your hands."

"What? Why?"

"Because I don't want you to fight me, silly."

Aaron blinked like he hadn't even thought of that, and he turned around anyway. His entire body shook as he put his hands behind his back. Missy put the gun in her pocket, trading it for large zip ties that she used like makeshift handcuffs before forcing Aaron back into the seat and facing her.

"Now I feel like I can trust you, so we'll leave the gun out of this for now."

The dog approached again, and Missy raised her hand as though she would hit it... and then it picked a small piece of Aaron's flesh off of the floor with a wet smack of its lips.

"Oh..." she said, voice quiet and delighted. "You want to help us clean up, do you?"

She made a kissing noise at the dog, coaxing it to her. Then she reached down and grabbed Aaron's mangled cock.

"C'mere, baby," she cooed at the dog, who approached and started licking the wound with a wide-eyed intensity.

"God, stop it!" Aaron screamed. "Please! What kind of sicko are you?"

"Talk about the pot calling the kettle black, huh? I'm the sicko? I just shot a guy who was feeding a human body to a pair of starving dogs. Who's the girl, hm? The girl in the buckets? Or is it more than one girl?"

"Just one girl. I don't know who she is."

Missy grabbed a deeper handful of his junk and squeezed, popping the testicle right out. It plopped onto the cushion, and Aaron screamed.

"Say her name."

"I—"

"If you don't know it, make one up."

"It's Alice. Her name was Alice."

The dog's licking had grown obnoxious, but Missy allowed it. She sat down on the couch beside Aaron and watched as the dog took the fleshy naked ball into its mouth and started chewing.

Aaron's screams were music to her ears.

"Slow down, sweetie. You'll choke." She reached down and patted the dog on the head.

"What did Alice do to deserve this? Did you kill her?"

Aaron's eyes were bloodshot, and all of the color had left his face. She wasn't sure how long he could hang on. The dog was tugging at his scrotum so hard that it jerked his body, then it moved on to grab his soft dick in between its teeth. Aaron's only reaction was a long, hard blink and a swallow that was so deep, he could have been digesting his own tongue.

"Nothing," he said, voice hoarse. "She didn't deserve it. I didn't kill her. They killed her. Donnie. He did it."

"Is that why you didn't fight me?"

She was curious. He hadn't so much as lifted a finger to try and stop her. He could have put up a fight, resisted, run... but he didn't. He just sat there and took it.

"I don't want to do this anymore," he sobbed. "I don't want to hurt people. I don't know how to stop. I want to get out. If you'll just let me go, I won't ever hurt anybody again. I'll leave town. I'll start a new life. I'll start over. There's still time to start over. It's never too late."

Missy cringed, looking over her shoulder at the kitchen. "Think Alice still has time to start over? Think she might be able to skip town and start a new life?"

Aaron squeezed his eyes closed in response, mouth twisting into such a pained expression that Missy nearly giggled with joy. He was torturing himself far more than she could.

A thump from the kitchen drew Missy's attention for a moment, and she saw the second dog had found its way over the gate and was plodding in to investigate what its companion was eating.

Missy sidled up closer to Aaron, tucking her body tightly against his. The second dog tried to push its way in, fighting the other dog for what little tissue remained on Aaron's groin. They snarled at each other, becoming a flurry of teeth and spittle.

"Oh, shhh. There's enough for everyone." She reached into her pocket and removed her knife, popping the blade out and using the sharp tip to raise Aaron's shirt to reveal his toned stomach.

"See, Aaron, this is where you're wrong. The problem isn't where you are or who you're with."

She dug the knife into his stomach, and he jerked backwards with a groan, chin falling to his chest as bloody vomit and saliva poured from his lips. She cut a slit there, then lay the knife aside to dig into the flesh with her fingers.

"The only good man is a dead man... because dead men can't hurt you," she whispered into his ear, teeth grazing the shell. She hooked her finger into a loop of his bowel before pulling it out and offering it to the second dog. It put its front feet on the couch and grabbed it.

Aaron rolled his head towards her, eyes fluttering as his body moved with the rhythmic tugs of the hungry dogs. She kissed him on the lips: metallic blood and the acrid tang of bile on her tongue.

"I'm sorry—" he whispered as the contact was broken. She wished he would scream again, beg her, beg God, even beg the fucking dogs.

Missy's eyes drifted down to the animals: watching as urine poured to dilute the blood from the mangled stump of his crotch, as shit and gastric fluid poured from the devoured bowels that were pulled like stubborn pasta through the widening gash in his stomach. She picked up the knife to make the hole a little wider for the beasts, and the layers of flesh peeled open like a zipper. She wiped the blood from the blade on his shirt and tucked the knife away in her pocket. The dogs lapped deeply at the blood that poured out, each one grabbing a different section of his intestinal tract so as to avoid another fight.

Missy cupped his jaw in one hand, rubbing her thumb across his mouth, where her black lipstick was smeared across his dirty face. "I just can't find it in me to care if you're sorry, and I won't give you the peace of forgiveness."

Eighteen

Tansi stared down at the number on the business card as her knee bounced nervously. She never thought she'd be calling Keistyn Ferrarese for anything, especially after the situation with Lucy. She knew that what happened was not at all the fault of Keistyn. After all, she was the only person willing to try to help them, but Tansi couldn't help but feel like she'd given them all a sense of false hope. Hope was not something they could afford; hope was dangerous and deceptive.

She was desperate, though, and the list of people she thought she could trust was slim. It wasn't even a list. She *had* to take this chance. She dialed the number and put the phone to her ear. It only rang twice before Keistyn answered.

"Keistyn Ferrarese."

"Hey, this is Tansi. I'm one of the girls from The Strip." Her voice lilted as though it was a question.

"Yeah, I remember. What you need?"

Straight to the point – Tansi appreciated that about her.

"I need your help. You know the other girl I live with?"

"Yeah, Alice. I remember her."

"I haven't seen her in…" Tansi paused, making a small croaking sound as the words were lost in her throat. She didn't even know how long it had been now. All she knew was it was *too* long. "I'm really worried about her. This isn't like her, and I don't know where she would be. She don't answer her phone, she hasn't been to the apartment, she don't have any money."

Keistyn was quiet on the other end.

"You still there?"

"Yeah."

"I know what you're thinking, but she wouldn't leave," Tansi insisted.

"Nah, Alice was a lifer. I know the type." Keistyn's voice sounded suddenly tired. "Has Sal been by to talk to you yet?"

"Sal?"

The name didn't ring a bell.

"The cop. The one I told you about."

"No, I haven't seen no cops."

"Alright. I'll see if he can come down there. He might be able to help."

"I don't talk to cops."

"Why'd you call me, Tansi?"

"What do you mean?"

"You called me because you want me to help you find Alice, right? I'm not a detective. This is what I can do for you. I'll have Sal meet you somewhere. Can I give him this number?"

Tansi reluctantly agreed, "Yeah."

"*Cooperate with him.*"

"Alright. Thank you."

"No problem. He'll be in touch."

Tansi expected it to be an agonizing day of waiting with the phone in her hand as she anticipated the call from Sal, but less than five minutes passed before her phone buzzed across the counter as she heated a cup of noodles in the microwave.

She picked up the phone with shaking hands, pressing it to her ear and clearing her throat.

"Hello?"

"Yeah, is this Tansi?" The voice on the other end was dismissive, the words rushed.

"Yeah."

"Key says I'm s'posed to come talk to you about some stuff. I'm in the area; I can swing by and pick you up in front of the apartments in five."

Tansi had a nervous twinge of fear in a deep place beneath her heart.

"We can stand and talk on the street. I don't got much to say," she said.

"I gotta eat breakfast, and I don't have time for all this shit, so I'm gonna kill two birds with one stone. You come eat breakfast or, hell, watch me eat fucking breakfast. See if I give a fuck. I'll be there in three now. Thanks, bye-bye now."

He canceled the call before his smart-ass mouth got out the last syllable. Tansi opted to stick a couple of twenties into her pocket instead of taking her entire purse, then tucked her phone into her opposite pocket.

By the time she went downstairs and emerged on the street, Sal was already parked out front. He was in an unmarked car, but all cops drove the same vehicle. Even when they thought they were being inconspicuous, it still screamed "pig." He had salt-and-pepper hair that was slicked back, cold blue eyes, and a bristling five o'clock shadow.

He chewed a piece of gum obnoxiously with his mouth open.

"Don't gawk, get in!" he yelled, one arm draped over the steering wheel while the other rolled to motion her over to him.

Tansi obeyed, getting into the passenger seat quickly. The car was in motion before her feet were off the pavement, and she swallowed a yelp in her throat as the momentum slammed the door shut. She looked over at Sal, who didn't respond to her reaction and continued driving. She tugged the seatbelt too hard and it caught, requiring her to let it relax and try again more calmly.

She pretended to text someone, keeping the phone tilted away from Sal as she typed out each street they turned on, just in case. Then she really did get a text; it was from Elijah.

> So I have a surprise for you. If I get you the address could you find a ride tomorrow? I can take you back home after. Show up around six thirty?

She typed out an affirmative response, for a moment forgetting where she was. She wondered if she could get a cab into town, but she knew they usually wouldn't pick up people on The Strip. It was thought to be too dangerous, too big of a risk of carjacking... or at least, that was the assumption.

The car jolted to a stop in front of a small diner. Tansi's mind spun for a moment as she tried to orient herself and where they were. She'd never seen this place before, but it was well lit and appeared to be in a decent area. She exited the car and followed Sal inside. He held the door open for her, and they chose a booth by a window.

A young waitress came over to take their order. She was obviously new, repeating each item Sal ordered as she wrote every letter onto her pad. He specified to split the checks.

"And for you?" she asked, turning her entire body towards Tansi.

"Oh..." Tansi blinked. She hadn't gone out for breakfast in so long, she wasn't even really sure what to order. "Bacon and pancakes. Is that okay?"

The waitress blinked back. "Of course it is. Do you want regular pancakes or something else?"

What other kind of pancakes were there?

"Regular is fine."

Tansi picked at her fingernails, only glancing up at Sal every so often. She wanted to get a good look at him, but she also didn't want him to catch her looking. The door behind her chimed several times and people filed in to get breakfast or an early brunch in a steady stream.

"So Key says you got a friend missing. Is she a prostitute too?"

Tansi stiffened, cheeks heating. She could feel the presence of someone sitting at the table behind her, and the inside of the cafe was bustling with life.

"She's a sex worker, yeah. I haven't seen her in days. It's not like her to do this. She isn't responding to texts or anything. I just wanna know she's okay – I don't care where she's at or what she's doing."

Sal sipped his lukewarm coffee, disinterested in her words. His eyes were shifty, darting around the room in paranoia. He laced his fingers together, clearing his throat as he forced a smile and a quiet and croaky "hey, how ya doin" to a man who walked by to sit somewhere behind them.

"You know this Alice girl's real name?"

"No," Tansi admitted. Alice had never liked to talk about her life before. Tansi didn't know anything about her.

"Alright, I'll look into it. See what I can do," Sal said, lifting his elbows away from the table as the waitress returned to set the plates in front of them. "Now, let me ask you some questions. A kind of 'I scratch your back, you scratch mine.'"

Tansi picked up a piece of greasy bacon between her fingers, biting just the end of it off as she chewed slowly. She nodded but couldn't help wondering what she could possibly do for him.

"Do you know anything about a new girl, maybe working under another pimp, who fits this bill?" He pulled a folded photo out of his pocket, laying it on the table and sliding it across to her.

It was a grainy black-and-white photo, clearly pulled from a security camera, which told her that the photo wasn't from The Strip. There wasn't a single CCTV or security camera on Jessop Terrace, not even in Pink Panther or the Flaming-O. It could just as easily incriminate the owner as it could prevent a crime. This photo was a shot from somewhere up high, maybe a street light, and it faced a stretch of sidewalk she didn't recognize. There were three people in the photo. One was a tall man in black – she assumed a bouncer or bartender because he was dragging another man, and Tansi was pretty sure it was DJ. Trailing behind the two, cloaked conveniently in shadow, was a woman in a black dress.

Tansi swallowed the small piece of bacon which, in her nervous state, could have been made of knives. She tapped her finger on DJ's chest.

"Is that—"

"Yeah," Sal said impatiently, as though there was no doubting the fuzzy representation's identity. "But I'm asking about *her*."

He mimicked her, tapping on the woman in the photo. Tansi tried to act like she was studying the woman: squinting and pulling the photo closer to her.

"Hard to see her," she finally remarked, pushing the picture back in Sal's direction. "Where is this?"

"Outside a bar on Kohlver Avenue."

"I know the one. DJ went there pretty often."

"So the girl."

"I don't know her, from what I can see. None of our girls would be over on Kohlver; not our jurisdiction, you feel me?"

Sal was growing even more impatient, although Tansi hadn't thought it possible. She glanced down at the photo again and back up at him.

"You don't think some girl killed DJ, do you?"

Sal narrowed his eyes at her. "I didn't say that. Do you have some reason to think some girl killed him?"

Tansi shrugged. "You're the cop."

Just like that, Sal was infuriated. He leaned in towards her, hissing his words so forcefully that spittle formed on his lower lip. "Listen, you useless fucking whore. I don't know why you'd want to protect this woman, but if you know something, I suggest you tell me now. If we find out otherwise, it's going to be bad news for you. The kind of bad news your friends have had lately. Right now, you're still worth a little more than the trouble you've been."

We, he'd said.

"You're working for Donnie," Tansi breathed.

"Working for him?" Sal scoffed, suddenly more offended than pissed. "I've been taking a cut of this Strip for decades. Let me make it clear to you: I don't give a fuck about DJ. I don't care that he's dead. I've always thought he was a pansy-ass, arrogant, son-of-a-bitch that was a huge liability. I do care if somebody is trying to dismantle everything we've worked for. I know the girl in this picture was there when DJ was killed. If you know who she is, tell her she's got one chance to tell us who offed him, and if she cooperates, we won't punish her. Hell, we'll give her a reward."

"Why you so sure that this girl was involved? She could've been somebody just walking down the street at the wrong time. Where's the bartender take him?"

"The bartender said he put him in the girl's car: newer model Cadillac CT5, black. Can't imagine many of those are driving around out here.

She took him to the parking garage on Blackstock and Western and met up with whoever killed him. We know the girl saw it happen because DJ had a like... kiss mark. You know, a lipstick print on his forehead."

Sal touched himself in the center of his forehead, "And Aaron had one on his cheek."

Tansi jolted.

"AJ?"

"Oh, yeah. Guess you didn't know. Somebody killed Aaron too. His damn dogs ate him to the bone from the waist down. Fucking mess. We got to get ahead of this thing because whoever it is might come after Donnie next, and he's getting a little— well, he's getting a little antsy."

"Listen, I don't know what you want me to do," Tansi whispered, exasperated. The waitress set down two checks on the table between them. "I don't know this girl, and I don't know nothing about no guys putting hits out on nobody."

"All I'm saying is talk to some of the other girls, see if they can give you any info. You get any intel, and there's a reward in it for you too. This girl is probably someone with a lot of abuse, probably from her daddy or something. Wanting to get back at men however she can. It's typical of these broads."

"Does Keistyn know you're a dirty cop?" Tansi asked, voice hesitant. She wanted to know, but *did* she want to know?

Sal scoffed again. "Nah. I'm the only cop that'd give her the time of day. If you try to tell her I'm working both sides too, I'll have you clubbed like a baby seal, got it?"

He thumbed money out of his wallet, laying it in a wad on top of the bill. He stood, leaving Tansi sitting with her cold and uneaten pancakes. Behind him, a woman in a black leather jacket and jeans stood and walked towards the door and out onto the street. The most subtle aroma of familiar perfume reached her nose, and she thought she recognized the woman's dark hair and build, but she couldn't see her face.

Sal noticed something had drawn her attention, so he started turning around.

"What about Alice? Are you going to try to find her?" Tansi blurted out, regaining his attention until the woman was clearly out of sight. She couldn't be sure, but she would have bet it was Missy. But *why*?

Sal huffed a laugh. "Yeah, sure. I'll let you know if she turns up."

Nineteen

Tansi's feet hurt after walking from Jessop Terrace to the bus stop just two streets over. It was in a part of Sunning that wasn't much better than The Strip, but she could still get a cab. She leaned against a lamppost and put in her location on the app for the cab to pick her up.

She absentmindedly tugged on the bottom of her shirt as she waited. It wasn't until she was trying to dress to impress that she realized how limited her closet was. Most of the items she had were made to draw attention, to show as much skin as possible, or to be easy access. Tonight ,she'd put on a nice pair of jeans and a nice top that covered her stomach. She wore a pair of sneakers for her walk but carried a pair of wedges to change into before she got there.

The car matching that of her driver pulled up, and she popped into the backseat. The car was clean and well kept. The man was probably in his fifties and wore a newsboy cap cockeyed on his head. She smiled at him when he glanced in the rearview mirror to nod at her.

She kicked off the sneakers and smashed them into her oversized purse, which could convert into a small backpack, and then she slid her feet into the platform shoes, lacing them up as the car moved along the road.

"Got something important you're going to, miss?" the man asked.

"Kind of," she said with a smile. "A friend invited me to... something. It's a surprise."

She didn't know why she was telling him this, but she was giddy and wanted to *enjoy* it. She wanted to displace herself from her real life for just a little while, as long as she could.

"Well, call me your fairy godmother." He laughed. It was a hearty, warm sound. "This chariot will arrive in five minutes, m'lady."

"Thank you," she breathed, running her fingers through her hair as she tried to add body to it. It was still damp underneath from her shower, and she wished she'd taken the time to dry it more. "Do you know what's at this address? Nothing came up online when I tried to look."

In reality, she hadn't had the data to do a good search. She was already going to have to pay extra for downloading this app to arrange a ride to and from the address.

"I've been by a few times, but I'm going to be honest, I don't think I've ever really looked," he admitted. "It's in a kind of upper side of town. You know, a little more ritzy than the rest of Sunning. Lots of organic smoothie shops and vegan sushi bars... Can sushi be vegan? Well, you know what I mean."

She leaned against the car door, watching the lights zip by as the car coasted along the street. She pretended a little adventurer was running through a temple, jumping over obstacles as he ran at the speed of the vehicle. It reminded her of being a kid in her parents' car when they went on vacation.

Tansi knew what the driver meant when they pulled down the street where her destination lay. Her eyes scanned the buildings that lined the pristine sidewalks until the car pulled up in front of one of the establishments and stopped.

"This is where I leave you," the man said, exiting the car and leaving the door standing open. She was suffused in yellow from the dome light above her, and the driver opened the rear door for her. He took off his hat and tipped his bald head.

"You're just—" Tansi had to stifle a laugh, "—too kind."

"Enjoy the rest of your night," he said, shutting the door behind her. "Don't forget to rate me on the app."

"Five stars," she proclaimed, blowing him a kiss.

He caught it in the air over the top of the car just before he dipped inside and drove away. She took a deep breath and turned around, looking at the building where she'd been dropped off. It was nestled between other storefronts similar to it on both sides but was set apart by its black brick exterior, with stark white trim, and mostly empty interior.

Was this the right place?

She slowly approached the door, noticing as she came closer that the suite wasn't empty at all. There were several temporary walls put up, and on each of them hung various types of artwork. People milled around inside, stopping to view each piece.

Her heart thrummed in her ears – buzzing and vibrating more than beating – as she opened the door and stepped inside.

A man at the door asked for her ticket and she shook her head, jaw dropping, to tell him she didn't have one.

"Oh, you're the girl Reilly has a ticket for, right?"

"Yes, that's me," she confirmed with a smile. "Tansi."

"Enjoy the show," the man said, motioning her inside.

Her eyes scanned the people milling around, but she didn't have to look long. Elijah emerged from around a corner and approached her.

He was positively beaming and dressed in black slacks with a black button-up shirt. She suddenly felt underdressed, only comforted by his perpetually messy hair and the still visible sleeves of tattoos on both arms.

"Hey."

It was all Tansi could manage to say, surprised when he wrapped his arms around her and squeezed. He led her around the maze of walls to one towards the back corner of the room.

"I've got something I want you to see," he said as they approached the wall.

"Is this an art show?" she asked. She had seen art galleries in movies, and they were kind of like this. She remembered that Elijah had said that he was also an artist.

"Yeah. The lady who runs it offered me a couple of spots, so I have some pieces scattered around, but I want to show you this one in particular."

He put his hands on her shoulders from behind, centering her before a canvas in the middle of the wall. Her heart all but stopped as she realized it was her. The painting was mostly black, rimmed in shadow, with silhouettes that were barely visible, if not for their subtly darker shade. On the right-hand side, a figure stood on stage, the black taking on a bluish tone. The figure had no features – just a small person in the dark – but she could tell that it was Elijah. And on the left, she sat with her back to the bar, light shining down on her: the only illuminated part of the image.

"What do you think? I usually do more surrealism-type stuff, but I was inspired—"

She turned around and kissed him, tears budding in the corners of her eyes. He was surprised at first, but kissed her back.

"You like it?" he asked, donning that ridiculously adorable grin.

"I love it," she confirmed, aware that she was blushing, and there was nothing she could do about it. "Can I see the rest of your work? The stuff you usually do, like you said."

"Of course," Elijah said, taking her by the hand as he guided her through the room.

He didn't just show her his artwork; he stopped at the pieces made by people he knew (some that he liked and some that he loathed). The art varied, from the bizarre and absurd to such photorealistic paintings that she thought they had to be from a camera. Elijah's pieces were strange but interesting. He explained them to her, how he had been inspired and how long it had taken him to create them. They spent over an hour browsing through the entire gallery.

The last painting was one of a dead bird. It was more realistic than the others, and she noted that the bird was half-decayed: poised like those velociraptor fossils in the pictures. Its blue and black feathers still clung to its wings.

"I've done this one twice," he explained. "The first one was destroyed in a fire, but the lady's sister wanted another one for her business lobby."

"It's kind of weird, isn't it?" Tansi asked. "Wanting a picture of a dead bluebird?"

"Yeah, it's weird. I've been commissioned to do weirder though, if I'm honest. One lady wanted me to paint a portrait of her nude, but she wanted her breasts to be clementines and her—" He looked around, smiling awkwardly at an elderly lady that walked by. "—you know. *That* to be a dragonfruit. She wanted to be held by a massive gorilla."
Tansi snorted.

"I'm not here to kink shame. Some people like being tied up; some people like gorillas eating their fruit."

"Thank you for inviting me to this," Tansi said, motioning around her. "This is amazing."

"I'm so glad you came, Tansi."

She winced, and his brow furrowed.

"Can I ask a weird favor?"

"Of course."

"Could you call me Charlie?"

Elijah's lips tugged into a small smile. "I'll call you whatever you want me to."

"I'm not ready to explain it yet. I hope that doesn't weird you out or anything. There's just a lot about me and my past, and I'm not sure how you're going to feel about it when I tell you."

He reached out and grabbed her hand. "I don't care where you've been. I'm here to meet you wherever you are right now, Charlie. "

Now it was her turn to have the dumb grin on her face. She couldn't say anything other than "okay" in a breathless sort of way.

A woman approached Elijah from behind, gently tugging his elbow. "I'm so sorry to interrupt, Mr. Reilly. Can I steal you for a second? I have a few people who want to talk to you about your art."

"Of course, give me just a second," Elijah said with a nod. The woman flashed Tansi a brief smile before walking away.

"I gotta go deal with these people," he sighed, voice apologetic.

"I may go home. You need to do your thing here, and I'll just be in the way. I'll message you? Maybe we can meet up for milkshakes again or something?"

"I'd love that. Be careful getting back home."

"I will. Bye."

She added the farewell awkwardly before heading out the door to the street. Everything seemed brighter, even at the late hour. She thought she might walk a couple of blocks before calling a cab, just to enjoy the night in this part of Sunning. She didn't look forward to going back to Jessop Terrace.

Tansi didn't get far in her shoes, feet aching. She stopped at a bench and sat down, pulling her sneakers out of her bag and swapping them out with the other shoes. As she sat there, she was aware of a car pulling up next to the sidewalk in front of her. It was a weird feeling when she wasn't "working," and it set her on edge before she even looked up and saw who it was.

"Need a ride?" Missy asked, leaning over to see out of the passenger side window.

Tansi could have fainted. Her head swam, and she wasn't sure she could speak at all. When she managed to respond, her voice was just a croak.

"No, I'm good. Thanks."

"Get in the car," Missy insisted.

"No, I don't need a ride," Tansi snapped, pulling her purse closer to her body as she got to her feet.

"Who's the guy?"

Everything stopped. She wasn't even sure the world was turning anymore. Tansi noted the devious smile that played across Missy's dark lips. Had she been stalking her? How did she know about Elijah?

She had to get in the car, she had to make sure that Missy knew that Elijah was a good guy, and she had to make sure Missy didn't have any reason to want to hurt her or him.

Tansi reluctantly slid into the black car, sitting on the farthest edge of the seat.

"So," Missy asked again, car in motion, "who is he?"

"Who?" Tansi asked. "There were a lot of guys in there."

"You know which one. The one from the bar, the one who took you out for ice cream, the one you kissed just a minute ago."

Tansi faltered, she didn't know what to say. Fear overtook her, and she thought she might cry even against her determination not to.

Missy's voice was playful somehow as she went on, "The guy who works at the hospital, who walks to his motorcycle in the parking garage with his headphones on like the ignorant and careless person he is. He never even notices me. Sometimes I like to see how close I can get... but sometimes, if I get a little too close, I just can't control myself. You have to know your limits."

Tansi was shaking. Not only had Missy been stalking her, she'd been stalking Elijah too. She tried not to show any sign of the fear that held her. She thought Missy would see it as a weakness. She bet she fed off that shit.

"You were at that diner, weren't you?" Tansi finally asked.

Missy smiled. "You're smarter than you look."

Tansi dipped her head.

"He's a dirty cop."

"You think I couldn't tell?"

"I appreciated you not telling him what you knew about me. Not that it would matter. This isn't my car, I picked it up from a guy in Bornemuth, Connecticut. He didn't need it anymore. Farthest north I've ever gone, then wandered back down to Tennessee. Stuck some Tennessee plates on it... obey all the traffic laws."

"Did you kill AJ too?"

She scoffed. "He might as well have killed himself. Boring. No fight in that piece of shit."

Tansi hated the next question that came out of her mouth, but she had to know.

"Who's next?"

"The cop, of course."

"Please don't. He's trying to help me find Alice. He might be dirty, but he's got resources. Just give him time to get me a lead."

A stoplight turned yellow ahead, and instead of trying to go through it, Missy slammed on the breaks. The car lurched to a stop at the line. Missy reached over, popping open the glove box and reaching inside. She withdrew a crucifix necklace.

Tansi clamped one hand over her mouth, taking the necklace with the other.

"Where did you get this?"

Missy yielded to traffic before turning right on red, heading down the last stretch to Jessop Terrace.

"Aaron's place. Your friend was cut into pieces, being fed to his dogs."

Tansi's stomach reeled, and she leaned forward, as though she could catch it and keep it from tumbling inside her. She felt a groan in her chest as her body threatened that it would be sick.

"Do not vomit in my car," Missy commanded. "I'll make you eat it off of the floorboard."

Tansi took several deep breaths through her nose, blowing the air through her lips as she talked herself through the nausea.

"I just want you to understand that you can't trust a man... any man. This guy from tonight, he's just like all the rest of them. He may hide it better than most, but it's there, lurking beneath the surface. You understand, don't you?"

"You're crazy," Tansi whispered.

"I'm *enlightened,* and you will be too, in time. I want you to know that you can trust me. Do you trust me? Because I want to trust you, but this goes both ways. So do you trust me?"

Tansi wanted to scream "no," but she knew better.

"Of course, I do," she responded.

"Then show me."

"I didn't tell the cop about you, right?"

Missy didn't respond.

The car pulled down The Strip and came to stop right in front of the apartment.

"I'm almost done here," Missy said as Tansi unbuckled, "just a few more things and I'll be moving on. I want to leave this place better than I found it, though. It's been one of my favorite spots. Maybe I'll come back."

Tansi hurried out of the car, afraid Sal might be lurking and see her with Missy. The car pulled away, and she stood on the sidewalk for several moments, chest heavy. She succumbed to the sickness and vomited in the street.

As much as Tansi was hoping the cop didn't see her, Missy was *counting on it*. Her eyes flicked to the rearview as the unmarked car, parked just down the street, flipped on its headlights , crawling along just far enough behind that it didn't seem immediately suspicious. Missy had been watching this man, though. He wasn't as clever and sneaky as he thought he was. She knew he had been watching Tansi's apartment, hoping to catch her talking to the men who had killed DJ and Aaron. She knew he had been the cop to investigate all of her murders here, and he never quite followed protocol on reporting the crimes.

When she had followed him to the diner with Tansi, she knew that he had to die, too. He was too nosey and too close to her big target: Donnie. She didn't want him to get in the way or to cause Tansi any further grief. She had been so pleased when she heard the girl play dumb.

Now that she had him on her tail, she just had to figure out how she was going to take him out. He could be seduced on a normal day, she supposed, but today he was looking for blood and not pussy. In some ways, that made him even more vulnerable, but he would probably be armed.

She pressed the gas to accelerate the car, keeping a close eye on his movements. He still hung back a little ways, and she knew that the distance would be her only opportunity. He was expecting a man in the car, not her. He had witnessed Tansi get out of the front seat at

The Palace. Missy turned down another street with little traffic and no pedestrians. Foot traffic in these areas came with a death wish.

A light ahead turned yellow, and she gunned it to get through. The red light caught her halfway through the intersection and someone honked, but the cop stayed behind at the line. She turned into an empty parking lot and opened the door. She left it standing open and got into the backseat, lying down on her side, and she waited.

The sound of tires on gravel and a flood of bright lights from behind the car let her know that the cop had taken the bait and was pulling up to check out the car. Missy remained totally still as she saw him pass the rear window.

"Dammit. Motherfucker took off," he muttered at the open door, growling in frustration and kicking the glass fragments on the ground.

Missy made a noise in her throat, feigning a voice full of delirium and pain. "Hello? What— what's going on?"

"Shit," Sal muttered, leaning across the seat to look at her.

"How did I get back here?" she asked, propping herself up on an elbow. She hissed and winced, putting a hand to her temple. "My head is killing me."

Sal circled around to the back door, leaning forward as he tugged the handle. Missy pulled both legs to her chest and kicked with every ounce of strength she had. Her feet struck the door so squarely and firmly that shockwaves of pain radiated up her legs and into her knees.

The pain was nothing compared to the satisfaction she felt when the top of the door hit Sal right in the face, though.

Sal stumbled backwards, tripping over his own heels and falling to the pavement in surprise. She launched herself out of the car, clearing the space between her and Sal as quickly as possible. If he regained any kind of control of his senses or awareness of what was going on, she was dead.

Missy was just about to reach for the knife in her pocket when her eyes fell on a sizable piece of pavement that was broken off and laying near Sal's feet. It was likely what he had fallen over as he had stumbled backwards. She grabbed it and slid atop him, skinning her knees on the asphalt.

She took the clump of rock in one hand and swung it into the side of Sal's bleeding face, knocking him back down to the ground as he tried to sit up. His shirt rode up on his stomach, revealing a gun in a holster. She set down the rock long enough to fumble for the weapon: flipping back the hood, then pressing the release to slide the gun out.

Sal grappled at her face, and she tossed the gun to the side, snarling at him as he grabbed a handful of her hair. She scrambled for her rock again, slamming it into his left knee. She felt his grip slacken and repeated the blow until he was wailing. He flopped back onto the ground, rolling onto his side to clutch at his knee. Missy started pummelling his other knee from the side. The stone made easy work of his patellas, crushing them until his pants were damp with blood.

She discarded the rock and stood, head spinning with distress. That had been a little close, she'd admit. She wouldn't admit, however, that she had ever lost control of the situation.

"You fucking bitch!" Sal barked, still clutching his knees and screaming.

Missy grabbed the thrown gun, turning off the safety and pointing it down at him. He sobered immediately, face still wet with tears and sweat, brow still pulled low with residual anger.

"Crawl," she said, motioning to his car.

"I'm not going to do shit," he snapped, spitting on the ground between them.

"Crawl, or I'll shoot you right here, right now," Missy said coolly.

A car drove by but didn't even slow down as it passed them. Missy kept a close eye on it as it continued down the street, keeping Sal in her periphery. People in this part of town must either not care, or they knew better than to put their noses in the business of other people—specifically people with guns.

"I'll ask you one more time to crawl. I don't have a lot of patience, and I have a lot of other things to do," Missy said with a sigh. "Crawl to your car. Passenger side."

Sal rolled over onto his stomach, dragging himself and his ruined knees across the uneven pavement.

"Oh, you've really done it, you crazy bitch. You are going to regret this. You are going to pay for this! Do you know who I am? I'm a fucking cop, and I will put you six feet deep so fast, I won't even need a shovel."

"Oh, big man. Making a lot of noise, aren't you? I am *so* scared." She panted, breath heavy, voice high pitched.

The mockery only made Sal more furious.

"Lie on your stomach, hands behind your back," she demanded as they approached the car.

Sal obeyed, lying just on the other side of the car. Missy swung the door open, putting one foot on Sal's back as she leaned inside the vehicle.

"Familiar position, isn't it?" Missy purred, jerking open the glove box and digging through its contents.

She found a pair of handcuffs, which was exactly what she was looking for. It didn't even matter that she didn't have the keys; she wouldn't need them. Then something caught her attention on the floorboard.

She briefly abandoned the cuffs in the seat to grab the thin book from the floor, holding it up in her hands. It was a children's alphabet book.

Missy laughed. "Oh, Sal. Want to learn your ACABs? Oh... wait. I mean ABCs? God, the thought that something like you has reproduced is discouraging."

She threw the book into the backseat and grabbed the cuffs again, using them to secure Sal's hands behind his back.

"How many kids do you have, Sally boy?" She asked.

"Two."

"Boys, girls?"

"Both girls."

"Thank God. There's some hope yet. What about you, though? Did you have any siblings? Your parents still alive?"

"No siblings." He groaned, face flat against the ground. "Mother is still alive."

Missy removed her foot from his back, squatting down beside him and trying to lift his chin with the handgun. He shied away from it.

"Your mama is probably sitting at home, pouring herself a cup of evening coffee, and doesn't even know her only baby boy is laying out here on the pavement." She tsk'd. "On your knees, now."

"I can't, they're fucking busted, you crazy whore."

Missy rolled her eyes. "Whore, bitch, cunt, slut. So predictable. Speaking of... you were wrong— about me, I mean. I was never abused. My adoptive father loved me. He never laid a hand on me or my mother or anyone else. That's typical of a man, though, to think that the only way a woman has any power, any grit, is when a man gives her that kind of trauma. Whether it's through some delusional savior bullshit or abuse, it's always given to us by you."

Sal rolled over, away from her, shoes hitting the bottom of the car. He stared up at her, directly in the eyes. Missy didn't like it. It was unsatisfying, even being in power over him. She wanted him to be afraid.

"We gonna get on with this, then?" Sal asked. "Or are you just going to stand there and talk until I die of old age down here?"

"You're right," she said, crouching down until she was straddling him. "Let's put that mouth of yours to better use."

She held the gun up, barrel to the sky as she ran her tongue up the side, then she spit on the end of it before offering it to his mouth. He shook his head, pursing his lips closed. If looks could kill... she'd be a dead woman.

She pressed it more firmly to his lips, the metal forcing itself against his front teeth.

"Open up." She pouted. "I don't want to have to go back to tend to your kneecaps."

He reluctantly opened his lips as she leaned back, hips rocking to put pressure on his thighs just above his mangled patellas.

"There we are. See? It isn't a dick, you don't have to take it so hard... but I want you to pretend it is. So suck it."

She pressed the gun deeper into his throat, feeling the notch of the front sight move from the ridges of his hard palate to the give of the soft. His eyes watered in response to the pressure.

Sal relented, making fists and banging them on the pavement as he moved his head forward and back on the barrel of the gun.

She knew he wanted to hit her. That was the power of the gun and not her own. This was another reason she didn't like to use guns. They were effective, fun in their own right, but they took the spotlight away from her. Sal wasn't afraid of her; he was afraid of the gun.

"Oh, so close, Sal," she cooed. "You look like you've done this before, huh?"

Sal's brow furrowed, and he took furious, shaking breaths through his nostrils as he increased the speed that he took the barrel.

Missy laughed, faking a moan, "So close. Right there, right—"

She squeezed the trigger, and the back of Sal's head bloomed open, the moist splatter of brain matter and blood leaving a bouquet of red on the pavement behind him.

"Oops."

His jaw locked around the barrel and she let his teeth grind against the metal before she allowed him to have it, dropping his head against the ground. She wiped the gun, hoping to rid it of any of her fingerprints. She wasn't on any books. She'd never been caught for any crime or applied for any job that required her prints, but it was always best to be safe. She lifted Sal's arm and squeezed his hand around the gun instead.

Missy stood, dusting her hands on her thighs before shutting Sal's door with her hip.

"Hope it was as good for you as it was for me, baby."

TWENTY

It didn't feel like a dream.

Maybe that was because she refused to let reality take that joy from her. They were in a house, and Tansi thought that it could be her grandparents' house but slightly different. The front door opened to a spacious yard in the middle of nowhere, surrounded by trees, with a long driveway that snaked off into civilization somewhere beyond.

Lucy sat on the front porch swing, and a little girl that looked just like her ran, laughing, in the front yard with a yellow lab. Alice was inside, fussing loudly about the shoes in front of the door.

Elijah was there, standing in the driveway. He looked back at her and smiled, waving over his shoulder. She asked where he was going, but he kept walking away. Tansi sprinted after him, and she felt like the farther she went, the more distant his form became, and the darker the forest closed in on her.

Eventually she was alone, and above the trees a pink-hued sky turned everything below the same tone; the forest was suddenly alive with the sounds of the city and not the desolate country. Then she saw the wolf. It was watching her from the cover of shadow, and Tansi was close enough to see the color of its eyes was the darkest shade of chestnut before black, smattered with green and yellow.

It was her. As Tansi backed away and then sidestepped to continue down the trail, the wolf's eyes followed her, but her head didn't move: a predatory way of tracking her prey. She had never realized how this behavior Missy displayed was *so* appropriate for an animal until she saw the wolf do it.

Then she started running. She returned to the farmhouse seconds later, but nothing was the same. Inside, Alice lay in a burned mass on the floor; the smell of charred flesh was overwhelming. It seemed that dream Tansi couldn't vomit, despite the nausea. Lucy was dead in the bathtub, soaking in blood that was so high that it nearly flooded over the rim.

In the kitchen, the trashcan rattled, and when Tansi reached for the lid it wailed like a baby. She didn't look.

Where was Elijah?

From another room trotted the orange cat from the alleyway – the one that Elijah had been feeding behind the Flaming-O. His legs were soaking wet, and he shook his little feet as he walked. He stopped in the center of the room, sitting down to lift his front paw to his mouth. As his rough tongue glazed over his curled toes, she realized he was covered in blood.

Tansi sprinted into the room where the cat had come from and found Elijah slumped in a chair: face stripped away, nearly to the bone. The walls were covered in horrifying artwork.

She heard the front door open and turned to look back into the main room. The cat had spun to face the door, his tail rising over his spine in a familiar greeting as he kneaded the rug and trilled at whoever was entering.

Tansi crept towards the bedroom door, leaning to peer around the corner with just her upper body. The floorboards creaked beneath her feet in the resounding silence.

Something lunged for her face.

Tansi sat bolt upright in bed, screaming. She was covered in sweat, and her heart pounded so forcefully that she thought it might burst through her chest and flee the scene.

"Sweet baby Jesus," she whispered.

Swinging her feet off of the bed, she sat on the edge, letting the tremors that went through her limbs lessen before she tried to stand.

She checked her phone: no messages since the last one she had received from Donnie. He had sent her a text earlier in the day, asking her to come by Pink Panther after close. It was now nearing four thirty, which meant the place had been shut down for a solid half hour.

She needed the distraction to keep herself from thinking about the financial predicament she was about to find herself in, anyway. Even though the last person she wanted to deal with tonight was Donnie, she knew she couldn't stand him up.

She had gotten complacent after her last payment from Missy, totalling over a thousand dollars. She thought it was probably more money than she'd ever had in her life. The problem was money only went so far, even that much money. She was paying for the apartment alone, since Alice was gone.

Dead – since Alice was dead. She felt like she hadn't fully processed the fact that the other woman wasn't coming back. Part of her wanted to believe that Missy was lying, but the other part of her had suspected it all along and now had that grim confirmation.

Without Alice, Tansi was paying out twice the amount for rent and utilities that she had before. She hadn't been working much, not since DJ wasn't around to make her. She was about to reach a point of desperation.

As though he could sense that weakness and vulnerability, Donnie had reached out.

She dressed for work, assuming it would suit anything Donnie could possibly want from her. Leaving the apartment left a wound in her chest, a creeping sickness as she walked across the street to Panther and its dimmed exterior. Inside, it still glowed gently with lights: the last embers of another night of business.

She found the front door unlocked, and the bouncer was nowhere to be seen. She knew that somewhere, one security guard still lurked. His shift would be over any time now, too. The cleaning crew came during the day, usually mid-afternoon. Donnie ran a tight ship.

She started up the stairs, anxiety mounting with each step. Behind her, the front door opened and she paused halfway up the stairs to watch it close, but no one was there. This only added to her stress and paranoia. Every other step, she stole another glance backwards to survey the empty dance floor.

Donnie's office door was open, and she could hear him as she approached the door. She slowed her steps to get as much of the conversation before entering as possible.

"Yeah, I got you a good one," Donnie said, sounding like he might be chewing something. "Front door is unlocked. You guys just come on in; you know where the changing rooms are. Yeah, I left it unlocked. Afraid of what? Who? Who's gonna walk in *my* establishment and cause problems? Get outta here with that bullshit. I'll lock up after you guys get here. Besides, I still got one guy downstairs somewhere. Maybe out back taking a smoke to milk the clock... I'll check in on the son-of-a-bitch. Alright, see you soon. Cash only, got it?"

Tansi hurried around the corner into the office as he ended the call. When she spoke, her voice was raspy and low, with less enthusiasm than she had intended.

"Heya, Donnie."

"Have a seat, Tansi," he said, motioning to the chair.

She treaded carefully across the glass floor like she always did. Something dizzying about walking across the clear elevation just didn't sit right with her. She collapsed into the seat, her fingernails digging into the curved edges of the arms.

"Enjoyed your little break?" he asked, opening a top drawer and pulling out a small stack of papers. "Hope so, because you know what they say: ain't no rest for the wicked. I crunched some numbers and got some stuff figured out. I am gonna need you here by nine o'clock Thursday through Saturday. That's three on, four off. Best schedule you ever had, huh?"

"What will I be doing?" Tansi asked.

Donnie's expression faltered for a moment and then he laughed.

"What do you mean 'what will I be doing'? You think I'm gonna make you a cocktail waitress or some shit?"

Tansi swallowed a lump of embarrassment in her throat but didn't respond.

"Let me level with you," Donnie said, his smile and laughter dissipating as quickly as it had come on. He leaned across the desk, lacing his fingers together. "DJ was more of a 'quantity-over-quality' man, you know what I mean? Everything he did was hard and fast, and he wanted to make the quickest buck he could. Bad businessman. I'm a *good* businessman. I'm all about the long game. People want quality. Those other girls—"

He fanned his hand in the air, and Tansi had to set her jaw to avoid saying anything.

"—Lucy, Alice. They were trash, let's be honest with ourselves. Nice enough girls, but when we're talking 'product,' DJ just didn't pick them right. I think you got potential, and you're young enough to get the hang of things and still have some working years left in you. I'll pay you well; don't you worry about that."

What was paying well in Donnie's world? Tansi wondered if she would still have to pick up working the streets on her days off or if Donnie would even allow that. She didn't bother asking, instead clearing her throat and gathering herself.

"Alright. When do I start? Next week?"

"Slow down there. I got something for you to do tonight. We'll call it a little initiation. I've got a couple of guys who were looking for a really unique experience. They're paying a lot of money to get a girl exclusively. They're probably already here downstairs. I got a room set up for you."

Tansi's hand reached up to touch her temple, surprised that her head wasn't actually spinning around atop her neck.

"What kind of experience? What do I have to do?"

"Listen, you're gonna do whatever the hell they want you to do. They're paying me good money, and I'll give you a good cut. They got two hours. What's the worst that could happen in two hours?"

Did he really want her to answer that?

"I'll take you downstairs," Donnie said, getting to his feet. He stood by the door, putting his arm out and bowing as she passed through.

"Madame," he quipped, "ladies first."

Just as Tansi feared, the room he escorted her to was the one directly under his office. It made her sick to imagine him thinking of her sexually, and to imagine him jerking off to whatever these two guys were about to do to her was even worse.

"Give me your phone and your keys," Donnie said, hand out-stretched.

Tansi hesitated.

"Give 'em here."

"I was just gonna leave them with my clothes in the corner," Tansi said, "that way you don't have to bother with keeping up with them."

Donnie didn't say anything else but made a "come here" motion with all of his fingers. Tansi relented, reaching into her pockets to withdraw her phone and her apartment key.

"Thatta girl," he said, clapping her on the back with his palm before he opened the door and let her inside. Tansi settled down on the chaise lounge, spreading her fingers across the fabric. It was lush: the darkest viridian, soft as velvet. It left traces of her hands when she touched it, and she drew a small heart in the fabric.

She wasn't sure what these guys would prefer: her in clothes, or her already undressed. This was a weird situation that she had never been in before. She opted to strip down to her underwear but left on her heels.

Tansi wasn't sure how much time she could handle waiting with the fear and anticipation that had taken over her thoughts. Just when she was about to get up and start pacing, the door opened. She heard the latch pop from the outside. She readied herself, taking a deep breath and putting on the mask of collected confidence.

Two men entered the room in silk bathrobes. They were both older, maybe in their sixties; she couldn't tell for sure. Even without their clothes on, Tansi could tell they came from money. There was something about the way their beards were trimmed and their hair was styled, the smell of the cologne that she knew came in a bottle that was worth more empty than most people's cars. That cologne had a way of lingering forever, somehow sinking into the man's skin and seeming to last far beyond its last use, like it had become part of their DNA.

She put on a smile like most people put on a hat, draping her arms across the back of the couch as she waited for them to close the door behind them.

"Hey, boys," she purred.

They stayed on the other side of the room, watching her for several moments, so she decided to take the initiative. Maybe this wouldn't be so bad after all. She could deal with a couple of shy guys; she knew she could make quick work of them. Pay for two hours; get twelve minutes.

She walked between them, pulling the belt of the robe on the man to her left. He put his hands on her hips, and she felt the man behind her run his hands up her arms and back down again.

On the second descent, he wrapped his arms around her, locking them behind her back.

Tansi faltered for a moment but then leaned into him. "Oh, you guys like it a little rough huh? I can—"

She was cut off by a fist flying into her face. Tansi saw stars and a rainbow of flashing rings. For the briefest moment, she blacked out, but the sensation of falling when the man behind her stumbled brought her back to the present.

"You can't do that," Tansi slurred, kicking out with her heels as the man in front of her approached again.

"We paid to do whatever we want," the man behind her whispered in her ear.

He hauled her off of her feet, dropping her back onto the couch and twisting her arms above her head. He was stronger than he looked, and she was still disoriented. Black snowflakes obscured her point of view, making it difficult to see anything at all. She could see the room and the limbs of the men on her periphery, but their faces were obscured by the dark holes in her vision.

As the other man tried to kneel on the couch, she waited until she felt his hands on her knees, trying to force them apart, and then she kicked out with all of her strength. She felt one of her feet hit its target, and the man started screaming.

She wrenched herself in the other man's grasp, trying to free herself. She felt her shoulders protest, the position threatening to dislocate them both if she didn't stop struggling.

If they wanted to play rapists, she was going to make sure they never desired to do so again. She was going to give them the experience they deserved.

Tansi pulled the man holding her arms towards her, and he stumbled forward, falling over the arm of the couch and onto her. She could feel his breath against her face, and she grabbed his lip between her teeth and bit down until she tasted blood.

He punched her in the stomach, in the ribs, grabbing handfuls of her flesh and squeezing as hard as he could. Tansi let go of his lip and used her freed hands to shove him with everything she had.

It wasn't enough. The second man came, and he hit her in the face again, this blow most definitely breaking her nose. She blinked frantically, trying to ward off the black cloud that was trying to take her to unconsciousness.

A loud screech echoed through the building, the hellish howl of a siren that sounded like a hellhound on a blood trail. Lights flashed overhead, and Tansi felt the sensation of rain falling on her upturned face, washing away pain with a wave of numbness.

The water pooled in her closed eyes, pouring through her lips onto her tongue, and she let herself go to that dark, quiet place.

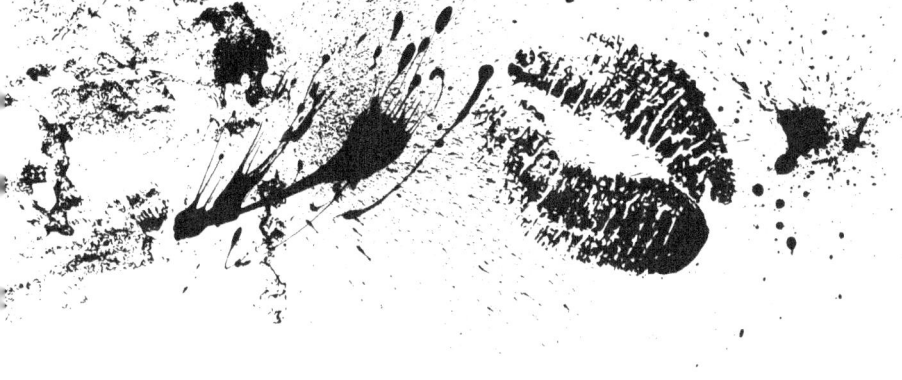

"Hey, you can't be up here."

The security guard kicked his shoe gently into Missy's side as she lay face down on the floor of the club box. One hand lay above her head, and one was pinned under her body, against her chest. He was a burly guy with broad shoulders and a military haircut. She was pretty sure the only combat he'd ever seen was when he was beating his wife.

Missy groaned but didn't respond to his nudge.

Her hair was over her face, but she could see his shoes as he stood there looking at her, likely trying to decide what to do with the straggler left at the club after hours.

She clutched the small knife against her chest, fingers laced tightly through the eyes of the handle. She was prepared to use it on him if she had to. She hoped he didn't notice the way her body tensed in preparation for action.

"I do not get paid enough for this bullshit," he whispered, flipping the pink neon lights off in the box before he left to leave Missy in the dark room.

The tight berber carpet was irritating to her cheek, intensifying that burning feeling in the most primitive part of her brain. Straining to hear the security guard as he went just down the hall, she heard him knock on a door or a wall, and then she heard him telling someone that a girl was passed out drunk in the club box. Although she couldn't make out what the other guy was saying, she heard the security guard say his shift was over and he was leaving.

She didn't know who was coming down the hall, but she hoped it was Donnie. She *prayed* it was him.

And it was.

"Hey." Donnie spoke from the doorway, voice echoing in the room.

Missy didn't move.

"Are you drunk, or are you dead?" Donnie grumbled, walking towards her. "I swear to God, if I gotta get rid of another—"

Donnie reached down to roll her over, and as her pinned hand was freed, she swiped at his calf. The first swipe was too low, striking the back of his shoe but allowing her next strike to be well-placed. She felt it slice through the thick tendons there, and Donnie collapsed onto the leg as though it were a crumbling pillar. She had to act fast. She was on her sore knees in an instant, cutting the back of his opposite heel and stabbing repeatedly,y just in case.

Missy got to her feet and walked to the seating to grab her purse. When she turned around, Donnie was back on his feet... well, one of his feet. He was dragging himself using one leg, although he screamed with every step as he hobbled out of the room.

She pursued slowly, in no hurry since he had turned towards the dead end on the elevated walkway. He fell into the wall, pulling the fire alarm before collapsing to the ground.

This was annoying. Missy was sure that on this end of town, Donnie wouldn't have an alarm that actually alerted any authorities, but that didn't mean someone wouldn't hear the alarm going off and call the fire department anyway.

Sprinklers came on and bright, pure white lights flashed. Missy was drenched before she even came to the fire alarm, and it looked like the slick surface of the metal platform had slowed Donnie down.

As Donnie dragged himself towards his office Missy took the time to stop and examine the fire alarm. She used her knife to forcefully rip the red cover off of the alarm, exposing the simple construct of the inner workings. She flipped the switch inside that had been triggered by the handle being pulled.

She was satisfied when the sound of the alarm subsided, and the sprinklers stopped soaking everything. The lights continued to flash, but that was fine.

As Donnie dragged himself inside his office, he tried to swing the door closed, but Missy caught it in her knife-wielding hand, forcing her head between the door and facing. She put on her best psychotic grin.

"Here's Johnny!"

She laughed at her own joke and forced the door open with her shoulder. It swung open and hit Donnie in the face. He reached up to clutch at his smashed nose.

"My nose!" he wailed.

"Did you know that line isn't in the book?" Missy asked, shutting the door behind her.

She cocked her head at the static light above her and the dryness of the room.

"Do you think your office is fireproof? Oh, Icarus, when you're flying this close to the sun..." she said with a sigh, dropping to her knees on the floor in front of him as he crawled backwards, dragging his legs. He propped himself up in a corner.

"You fucking bitch!" he snarled, and Missy mouthed the words along with him.

"Yeah, I know," she said with a crinkle of her nose. "I know."

"What do you want from me?" Donnie asked. "You want money?"

"I'm going to need your cooperation, Donald." Missy said, setting her purse on the desk. "I'm going to put you in your office chair. If you fight me... well, you're smart enough not to do that aren't you?"

She held up the hand that still wielded the trench knife, waving her fingers that held the knuckle duster. It was a pretty small blade, but wicked sharp, and it did its job just as well as her stiletto.

Donnie nodded. "Sure. I know how to cooperate. We can come to some kind of agreement, right? Mano a mano, eh?"

"Something like that," she said, standing and motioning to the chair. "Crawl over to the chair."

"Crawl?"

"Well, if you can walk, have at it," she snarked.

Donnie scowled at her, but he started crawling across the floor, making his way slowly around his desk. She helped hoist him into the chair and then took off the knife, laying it out of reach on the other side of the desk. She dug through her purse to find a roll of duct tape.

"What's that for?"

"Security," she said, pulling the end of the tape free. "It's this, or I can find the right tendon to make your arms useless, too. Up to you."

Donnie gritted his teeth, grabbing the edge of the chair arms as she wrapped the tape around his arm several times. Donnie lunged forward, grabbing a paperweight with his free hand and swinging it at Missy.

He missed her face but hit her on the shoulder. Missy paused, looking him in the eye as she taped down his opposite hand, first loosely as he fought, but then with increasing tension.

"Now you've just pissed me off." She sat on the edge of the desk and put her foot on the chair between his legs, pushing the chair away slightly. She rubbed her shoulder. "That really fucking hurt."

"Sorry, I lash out when I'm stressed sometimes," Donnie said, voice seething with sarcasm.

"Aw, see? We have something in common." Missy leaned forward, satisfied to see Donnie's expression show real worry for the first time. "You're lucky I don't shove your dick down your throat like I did to that other piece of shit."

Donnie's jaw dropped, face painted with streaks of beet-colored blood from his broken nose.

"You..."

"Yes, me. Him, that pussy Aaron, and that nosy cop."

"What's this all about? Did someone hire you? Are you working with somebody? The Huynhs? I can pay you twice what they're asking. Twice the price, protection, and a hefty sum, if you take my guys straight to whoever started this."

"I'm not into all of these petty squabbles and street politics. I'm here because you're... you."

Donnie paused, his mind working to figure out what exactly she meant.

"Is this about the girls?"

"It's always about the girls," Missy concurred.

"You gotta understand. It's not personal. I don't know you, I don't care about you. I don't care about any of these whores. Might call that ugly, but I call it honest. It's a man's nature to want power and control over the lesser sex."

Missy smiled, leaning over him with her hands on the arms of his chair as she locked eyes with him. She saw the fear in his eyes, and he saw

nothing but an obsidian reflection in hers: a shadow of himself, outlined
in black, with nothing inside.

"A man's nature? Baby, it's your *religion*."

She leaned back to reach into her bag and withdrew an aged hammer,
the rubber handle so mottled with grease that it could have been mis-
taken for black. There had been construction on an old building near
Koplin Grand, and one of the men had left his toolbag by the fence one
night. The hammer had glistened in the streetlight like it was beckoning
to her, a divine object that sought her out.

"What are you doing?"

His voice was shrill and held a fearful vibrato. She heard him jerk
against his restraints, and the chair bounced across the glass floor. She
seated herself on his desk, spreading her knees and arching her back. She
propped her elbow on her hip, letting the hammer in her hand dangle
from her loose wrist.

"I could have made this quick. All I asked for was cooperation. You
never had a chance to survive this encounter, but you had a chance to
suffer less."

She smashed his ring and pinky fingers on his right hand, raising the
hammer over her head and swinging until wood pieces flew off of the arm
of the chair. She paused, panting as she surveyed the pulpy remainder
of the two digits. Donnie was wailing, shaking the chair as he tried to
bounce away.

She used the claw end of the hammer this time, sliding his middle finger between the curved metal pieces, really having to force them around
the pudge of the finger below the joint. Then she pried up until the claw
touched the back of his hand and the finger popped free inside, swelling
and purple.

She tried to take the hammer off of the finger, but with the inflammation, it was stuck between the claws even tighter.

"It's really in there, isn't it?" she asked, tugging again, much to the dismay of Donnie.

"God, stop it!" he begged. "Come on, we have to be able to work this out some other way. I'll get out of town, I'll burn this whole fucking club to the ground. You name it."

Missy acted like she wasn't listening, again picking up the knife up and using it to saw the finger off at the dislocation. Donnie impressed her as he watched the amputation, face taking on an ashen pallor but never looking away.

She held up the hammer, her finger still stuck between the claws, but at least she could use it again.

"I borrowed this hammer," she explained. "I looked for anything else fun I could incorporate into playtime, but there wasn't much else. Except these... and sometimes, you know, it's the simple things."

She pulled out a handful of long nails, some rusted and some shining with newness. She stuck the fat end of one of them between her teeth, placing the sharp tip of another against the top of his left hand.

"Hold steady now. Wouldn't want to smash your finger."

She drove the nail through his hand with several taps, taking her time until the flat top was flush against his hand, then she did the same to the other side.

"I get why crucifixion was in for a while. This is so much fun." She giggled.

Missy then swung the hammer into the front of his knee. Nothing happened visually, any damage obscured by his pants. His leg did jerk up, though.

"Checking your reflexes," she explained. "My mom told me once that I would be a great doctor. What do you think?"

Donnie gritted his teeth, clamping his eyes shut as he whispered something that she couldn't make out.

"Getting a little bored here." She sighed, pushing the chair back so that she could stand. "What else can we smash..."

She looked down at Donnie's crotch, and her eyes lit up, "Why didn't I think of this before?"

"No, no, no!" he screamed, voice breaking.

Missy poised to swing the hammer again, but Donnie's body went limp. She stopped mid-swing, brow furrowed. She pushed the hammer against his chest. The chair rolled away from her and spun slightly, but Donnie didn't move.

She pulled his head up by his hair, but it was heavy in her hands. He had passed the fuck out. She dropped the hammer to the floor. This was no fun if he wasn't screaming.

"Gotta cut the party short, I guess..." She sighed.

She stretched out the rest of the tape, starting below Donnie's chin and wrapping his entire head tight. She noticed that he was rousing, his chest jerking as he struggled for breath through all of the layers of tape. He'd suffocate soon enough, but she wasn't quite done with him yet.

She took the remaining nails, hammering one through each eye with a firm whack.

"My placement is *impeccable*," she said to herself when the nails drove through his eyeballs with so little effort. The tape was harder to get through than the tissue beneath. "I really should have played Battleship more. I'm a natural."

Donnie's body writhed, vibrating against the chair as though he was having a seizure.

"Almost done…" she whispered, using the last few nails to make a (sort of) smile underneath the eyes. She leaned towards him, placing a firm kiss on the tape that covered his head.

Satisfied, Missy set to packing her things. Something caught her eye on the desktop as she prepared to leave: a key with a hangtag for The Palace on it, lying beside a phone.

Missy reached for it, lifting the phone to find that it had no passcode or lock. Her brows flicked upwards with interest, a smile pulling on the corners of her lips.

Twenty-One

Tansi struggled to wake, her head throbbing with pain. Lights flashed beyond her lids, illuminating everything red and pink before fizzling to black again. She slowly recalled what had happened before she had blacked out, her body attempting to protect her from the trauma that she had endured. The last thing she remembered was the rain. Rain?

Her eyes shot open, blurred with water. She realized her bra and underwear were saturated. The couch felt like a too-pregnant sponge. She realized it hadn't been rain at all, of course, but the sprinkler system. She tried to sit up, and her body felt like it was on fire. She leaned over, stomach aching with waves of pain. She let herself sob between her knees, staring at the floor.

Tansi looked up and noticed the door was standing ajar, leading to the hallway beyond. She struggled to her feet, every step sending a torturous shockwave through her body. As she walked out the door, her foot struck something on the floor.

She looked down and saw her phone and key lying there... along with a human finger. Tansi swallowed, eyes moving up the hallway, where she strained to see beyond the strobe of lights in search of the dark figure of Missy somewhere out there.

She'd been here; she knew it. She was surprised that she didn't even have a visceral reaction to the amputated digit on the ground. She reached down to pick up her things, clutching the phone and key like they were the only things keeping her alive.

She trudged across the wet dance floor, through the front door, and onto the street. The sunlight might as well have been a spike through her brain. She clamped her eyes closed, nearly falling to the ground as she stumbled across the road.

The Strip was a ghost town during the day. No one offered to help her. There was no one to see her dragging herself across the street in her underwear like a zombie. She couldn't go to her apartment and Flaming-O was closed – there was only one other option.

Hours seemed to pass before she reached the brothel. She collapsed against the front door, wrenching the knob between her desperate fingers. It didn't turn, though she hadn't really expected it to. She banged on the door with her fists, using every ounce of energy she had left.

The door opened, and she fell inside, caught before she hit the floor and pulled to her feet against someone's body.

"What is this?" Zahid's voice sounded annoyed, but he clutched her against him as he half carried, half dragged her into the room behind the desk.

Zahid lowered her onto the couch. Every sound felt like a physical touch to her synapses: the sultry voice of the man speaking in a different language on the soap opera playing on television, the beeping of something somewhere else, the tinkle of beads as Zahid came back into the room through the curtain in the doorway.

"I'm sorry," Tansi apologized as he lifted her head and put a pillow beneath it to prop her up. "I didn't know where else to go."

"What has happened to you? Tansi, right?" he asked, and she felt a breeze of cold air as he shook open a blanket on top of her.

"It's a long story," she groaned.

"Where are you hurt?"

Everywhere.

Everywhere.

"Open your mouth," he said and Tansi realized her eyes had been closed. She opened them, squinting at him as he held a couple of pills in one hand and a glass of water in another.

"What is it?" she asked.

"Something for the pain, it'll help you sleep, too."

She accepted the pills and swallowed them, drinking the water so deeply that it trickled down her chin.

"You will be safe here," Zahid confirmed, taking the empty glass as he stood and looked at the front counter. "No one will come through that door to hurt you."

"Thank you, Zahid. I promise I won't be here long. If I can just sleep a few hours... I'll be good, then."

Zahid smiled softly, barely visible through his thick black beard. He handed her a t-shirt and a pair of shorts.

"These belonged to my daughter. I think they should fit. If you will remove your bra and panties, I'll dry them for you."

Tansi sat up and took the clothes from him, clutching them in her hands as she repeated, "Thank you. Thank you for your kindness."

He scoffed. "It is not kindness; it is humanity. Are you hungry?"

Tansi pursed her lips together and started to decline, but he held up a hand to silence her and disappeared into an adjacent room.

She stood and stripped off her underwear and her bra, laying them across the back of the couch as she slipped on the shorts and shirt. She settled onto the cushions, criss-crossing her legs and covering herself with the blanket.

Zahid returned and handed her a paper plate full of steaming food: rice, chicken, and maybe spinach and eggplant. She wasn't sure.

"Leftovers... I was having it for lunch," he explained, like she needed to know.

"You said you had a daughter?" Tansi asked, blowing cool air from her lips onto a forkful of the dish.

Zahid sighed, sitting down beside her on the couch. He muted the television and stared forward at the wall. Tansi immediately regretted asking, swallowing down that regret and the food in the same gulp.

"She died five years ago," Zahid responded, lacing his fingers together in his lap. "She was shot, not intentionally. Driveby, maybe road rage, and a bullet hit her right in the temple. She died instantly. I lost my reason to live. Five years."

He stood up then, as quickly as he'd sat down. "I have a lot of cleaning to do before I unlock the doors. Get some rest and head out whenever you're ready."

"You're still here though, Zahid," Tansi called after him as he headed out the doorway into the lobby.

He paused, looking back at her, patting his fist against his chest. "Not here. Not here."

Twenty-Two

Tansi would have sworn on her life that the pills Zahid gave her had contained magic. When she awoke on his couch, she felt rested, and the pain had resolved to soreness and dull aches that throbbed with movement. She sat up, looking down at the map of black and pink on her stomach and thighs. The visual acknowledgement of the wounds seemed to rejuvenate the intensity of her perceived pain so she dropped her shirt back over them.

Her now dry undergarments were laid on top of the television. She retrieved them and put them on, spinning as she heard the buzzing of her phone. She'd been holding it in her hand when she stumbled in, but from that point, she didn't know where it had gone.

It buzzed again, and she feverishly tracked it between the couch cushions. She had a text from Elijah. She sighed in relief, flipping open the message stream. Her heart stopped at the message preview and her hands started shaking as she opened the message history.

Good night <3

Glad you came. Ice Cream soon?

please

Hey, you busy? I hate to even ask but I'm in Sunning and kind of stranded. Can you pick me up? I'm sitting in a parking garage by Sister's Automotive to get out of the rain.

It's pouring the rain. I'll be there in 5, just sit tight. I'll park my bike and we can take a cab together. That's a bad part of town, not a lot of traffic. Keep aware.

My hero.

Does he always talk this much or should I cut out his tongue?

Tansi had never felt such horror. Not in all that she experienced recently, not in any nightmare she had ever had. She hadn't sent Elijah the message about being stranded and needing a ride. She even tried to convince herself that maybe she *had* sent it.

The last message from Elijah, the one that she had just received, was the one that chilled her to the core. She couldn't breathe. It was as though she ceased to exist for just a moment before the heat and life rushed back into her.

Three more messages popped up, one right after another.

Looking for advice here.

So yes?

☒

Tansi started to type out a message but her hands shook so hard that she couldn't press the right letters on the keypad. Instead she dialed his number, holding it up to her ear. Someone answered on the other end, but they didn't say anything.

"Elijah?" she whispered, voice breaking with distress.

Nothing but silence.

She took a deep breath, closing her eyes. "Missy?"

"Hey, baby."

It was undeniably Missy's sultry voice that responded. Tansi couldn't control her sobs now, but she forced them to be noiseless. She couldn't give Missy that kind of satisfaction. She couldn't feed that power she craved, that fear she sought.

"You don't have to do this," Tansi whispered.

"But I want to," she said. "Don't you understand? You are such an ungrateful little shit, you know that? I came here and I did all of this for you."

"I never asked for this," she insisted.

"But *you did*. You wanted it, I could see it in your eyes. Not only that, but let's be fair... you literally asked for me to kill DJ. That makes you an accomplice. How did it feel to be responsible for that scum leaving earth? Didn't it feel good?"

"Elijah is a good man. He isn't like them."

"'Good man' is such an oxymoron... but he is a weak man, a soft man. Is that what you mean?"

"Where is he?"

"Somewhere *secure*. Let's call it... *safe*?"

There was a shuffling, and Tansi heard a distant groan. She covered her mouth to keep from screaming.

"If you hurt him... I swear to God, Missy, if you hurt him..."

"Hurt him? Oh, that's not even the start of it. Do you know what I'm going to do to him? I eat boys like this for breakfast. He's *nothing*."

"Please. Please don't take him from me," she begged, getting to her feet and leaving the building. She stood on the sidewalk, washed in pink from the growing night. She could feel the cool pavement under the soles of her feet.

Missy didn't respond, but Tansi heard the sound of a door closing. Maybe it was a car door.

"Why me?" Tansi finally asked.

She heard Missy exhale softly into the receiver as she released a small laugh. "Oh, honey, don't flatter yourself. I was bored, and you were available."

Tansi's mind fumbled for any way she could solve this. She didn't know where Missy was or where she was keeping Elijah. She needed to get closer, somehow. There had to be a way. She had to attempt to outsmart her, but Tansi just wasn't sure she had it in her.

"It'll all be over soon, and I'll be gone," Missy assured her.

"Wait," Tansi said, afraid that the other woman might hang up and never answer the phone again. "What if I... what if I need to do it myself?"

"Do what yourself?" Missy's voice held a curious tone, as though her interest was suddenly piqued.

"I want to understand. I feel like we have this connection, and I want to understand. I just don't. I need to get it."

"Tell me what it is you want to do," Missy repeated.

"I want to kill him," Tansi said. "I want to do it myself, I want to feel it. I want to feel what it is you feel, Missy."

There was a long pause, and Tansi thought her heart stopped in the silence.

"Where are you?" Missy finally asked.

Tansi let loose a shaky breath of relief. "On The Strip. I'm outside the brothel, standing on the street."

"I'm already on my way," Missy said, voice raising slightly. "I was hoping you might come around. I was hoping I could share this moment with you."

"I'm... so glad we can do this together. Thank you."

"I'll be there in ten."

The call ended.

Tansi didn't have a plan, but she was going to figure this out. Missy said she'd be there in ten minutes, but she arrived in five. The dark car rolled up and stopped alongside the sidewalk. Tansi gathered all of her courage and opened the door, getting in and buckling up.

Tansi didn't keep up with where they were going. Instead, she kept an eye on Missy as she drove. She was so calm, showing no emotion at all. It was as though she had never killed anyone and definitely wasn't holding a man hostage. How many of these people walked among the normal ones every day?

"Are you ever afraid?" Tansi asked.

"No," Missy responded, "I don't know what that feels like."

"Have you ever been happy?"

Missy looked over at her, dark gaze so reminiscent of the dream wolf in that moment.

"No. I don't know what that feels like, either."

The car slowed down in the middle of a street, and then it rolled to a stop. Tansi looked around, but nothing was nearby. No buildings, no people, no cars, no encampments. Missy stared forward, jaw clenching.

She was having second thoughts. Tansi's stomach flipped.

"I want you to know that you can trust me," Tansi said, repeating exactly what Missy had once said to her. "Do you trust me? Because I want to trust *you*, but this goes both ways."

Missy didn't physically react; she didn't look Tansi's direction.

Tansi's voice shook, but she tried to sound confident. "So do you trust me?"

Missy's jaw relaxed, and she let off the brake, easing the car down the street. Tansi tried to mask her sigh of relief, but it sounded so loud in the quiet interior of the car.

They were gliding down another empty street, this one with a sign that warned of a dead end. The end of the road birthed into a gravel parking lot, where lay a set of gates and a series of storage units. A sign on the gate warned that there were no security cameras, and any loss or theft was not the responsibility of the lot owner.

Missy opened the glovebox and withdrew a key with a number on it.

Sixty-seven.

Tansi watched as Missy exited the car and typed something in on a keypad that allowed the gates to open. It was a poor design, Tansi thought, to not be able to use the keypad from your car window. Missy got back inside, keeping the key clutched in her hand as she rolled through the rows of buildings. Straight ahead was a unit with the number sixty-five on it, and to the right were sixty-six through seventy.

"Knife or hammer?" Missy asked, parking the car. The lights bounced off of sixty-five's metal door, creating a harsh daylight inside the car.

"What?"

"That's the options."

Tansi swallowed nervously. "Hammer."

Missy sat for a few more moments and then pursed her lips together in satisfaction.

"Let's go, then."

Missy got out of the car, and Tansi unbuckled. Tansi watched as Missy started around the front of the car, and she dove into the driver's seat. It was now or never.

She jerked the car into gear so harshly that it groaned in protest and she looked up just long enough to see a look of genuine surprise on Missy's face before she mashed the gas pedal with her foot.

The car lurched forward, only able to go a few feet before it hit the woman and pinned her against the door of sixty-five. Tansi's head struck the steering wheel, but she recovered, wincing in pain as she slammed the car into park.

She walked slowly to the front of the car, watching as Missy growled and groaned against the hood, scratching the shining surface with her black nails. She still clutched the key in the other hand. Tansi reached over, jerking the key out of her weakened grip. She could see now that her body was pinched in half, and Tansi was sure if she backed up, Missy would just fall apart.

Blood poured from her nose and lips, but her expression was anything but hurt: it was furious.

"I don't trust you," Missy choked out quietly. "I never did."

She spit a bloody wad of mucus into Tansi's face.

Tansi wiped her face, jogging around the back of the car and putting the key into the door with shaking hands.

"Elijah?" she called into the door, struggling to raise it. "I'm coming. I'm here."

The door rolled open of its own power about halfway up, and the lights from the parking lot illuminated a storage unit that contained just a backpack and a box. Tansi rushed over, tearing the zipper open to find the bag was stuffed with money. The box had newspaper clippings and old license plates: knives, tools, rope, tape, bottles of liquid, boxes and tins... just junk.

Tansi rushed out of the unit, screaming her frustrations into the night.

"Where is he, you fucking psycho bitch?" she roared, chest and throat aching with the force.

Missy lay sprawled across the hood, cheek resting delicately against the surface, pupils fixed, full lips just barely open as blood continued to pour from them.

Sunning was over three hundred square miles, and she had no idea where to even begin looking.

She moved over to Missy's side, putting her hands against her cheek.

"Come on, wake up. You ain't dying that easy. Where is he?" She slammed her fists against the hood. "Where is he? God, please just tell me where he is."

Tansi fell to her knees, winding her fingers through her hair as she sobbed into the gravel, and it hurt *everywhere, everywhere.*

Printed in Dunstable, United Kingdom